Collect all the

Sam Cooper Adventure Stories™

by Max Elliot Anderson

Lost Island Smugglers
Captain Jack's Treasure
River Rampage

LOST ISLAND SMUGGLERS

Sam Cooper had just moved to Harper's Inlet when he met Tony. Tony's father owned a marina. Sam, Tony, and Tyler took scuba lessons together. Tony got them in for free. After they completed the course, the boys decided to try out their new skills in the real world...the ocean. The only problem was, no one had permission.

While Tony's father was away on a buying trip, the boys took one of the rental sailboats out for their diving adventure. Everything went well until the biggest storm Tony had ever seen blew up from out of nowhere, and the boys found themselves stranded on Lost Island.

But, if they thought the worst had happened, they were wrong. The boys discovered a secret hideout that was used by men in high powered speedboats.

Sam and his friends knew the men were up to something, only they didn't know what. They had to find a way to stop them, but how? And, even if they did, the boys could never tell anyone about it. Join Sam Cooper, Tony, and Tyler on their scary scuba, ocean, island adventure.

Tyler, Sam, and Tony

The Sam Cooper Adventure Series

LOST
ISLAND
SMUGGLERS

by

MAX ELLIOT ANDERSON

SharksFinn

A Port Yonder Press Imprint

Lost Island Smugglers
The Sam Cooper Adventure Series - Volume 1

Published by
Port Yonder Press LLC
Shellsburg, Iowa
www.PortYonderPress.com

ISBN 9781935600022
Library of Congress Number 2010924745

Editorial Team: Naomi Musch, Suzanne Hartmann, & C. MaggieWoychik
Illustrations by Holly Heisey
Book design by Aidana WillowRaven
Logo designs by Tony Lavoie

A SharksFinn Book: an imprint of Port Yonder Press

First paperback edition

Printed in the United States of America 2010

CONTENTS

Lost Island Smugglers

Max Elliot Anderson

CHAPTER 1

The Big Move

Sam Cooper's mouth dropped open as he watched a police SWAT team move in on a house not three blocks from his own front door. After surrounding that house, two officers smashed the door open as others swarmed inside with their weapons ready.

"I can't believe this is happening," Sam said right out loud.

"Maybe it's not so bad we have to leave this place after all," his mother answered.

Sam continued watching the news as a reporter said, "In a predawn raid, officers from local, state, and federal departments arrested six suspects in what they say is the largest drug ring our town has ever seen."

Next the police chief said, "We have to stop the flow of drugs at the source. By the time they get this far, it's already too late."

If I ever saw drug dealers, Sam thought, *I'd stop 'em.*

Sure, it was one thing to think that, but what if he were faced with the real thing. What then?

Sam Cooper was the kind of guy who could figure his way around almost any problem. But this summer he would soon be tested in a way that he could never have imagined.

He didn't know it now, but Sam was on a collision course with his greatest challenge yet, where his very life would be in danger. Somehow, he could feel it, even though he didn't know exactly what *it* was. One thing was sure; it would take everything he knew just to survive.

Sam loved adventure and a good mystery gave him goose bumps. So far, his life had been one move after another, never living in the same place for more than a short while. He had thought that was adventure enough.

But Samuel Clement Cooper was not one bit happy about moving *again*. He had already lost count of the many places he'd lived before, and he was only eleven.

It seemed he'd just get settled into a new school, make a few friends and then it was time to move on. His dad couldn't help it though. His job as a research biologist kept their family on the move. But for Sam, being the new kid at school was getting a little old.

Sam Cooper had sandy colored hair which he kept not too long, and not too short. He was muscular and athletic at the same time. Sam liked to wear golf shirts or T-shirts, long pants, and tennis shoes.

He had a solid quality about him. His friends knew he was the kind of person they could depend on. In fact, each time he moved, his friends seemed to take it harder than he did.

At least this time, Sam's family was able to wait until school finished before they made the move. Some years he had to change schools in the middle of the year. Those were the most difficult because he might be right in the middle of a great science project, a school play, or the team he played on had been enjoying a winning season. And Sam was often the main reason why.

This time he had the whole summer to find his way around the next town and make some new friends. *Maybe this next school year will be better*, he hoped.

He and his father worked together in the garage packing boxes as the family prepared for their move. Sam crammed a football, along with his favorite baseball glove, into a box marked "sports."

"Hey Dad," he asked, "will we ever be able to stop moving? Coach told me I was gonna play quarterback this fall."

"I'm sorry, Sam. I know this is hard on you, but there isn't much we can do about where my work takes me."

"What exactly will you be doing this time?" Sam asked.

"We'll be working in a place called Ten Thousand Islands."

Sam let out a long, loud whistle. "Are there really ten thousand of them, Dad?"

"I'm not sure. That's one of the things we'll be studying. It's part of the Everglades. We're going to see if draining the swampland so houses can be built has hurt the plants or animals there."

Sam wiped some sweat from his upper lip and sniffed. "Sounds a little boring to me. Nothing like the work you did in Alaska."

"I know, but at least in Florida we'll be warmer." Then he smiled. "No penguins anywhere near that place."

"Unless we go to an aquarium," Sam said with a chuckle. "How long do we get to live there?"

"My contract is for two years, but if all goes well, it could be renewed for at least three more after that."

This time Sam whistled even longer and louder. "Five years. I don't know what I'd do if I got to live in the same place for five whole years."

His father stopped packing for a moment. "I know. My job makes it tough on all of us. I truly am sorry about that. But I don't have much choice except to go where the work is."

"It's just that I have such a hard time making new friends."

"You?" his father asked in surprise. "I can't imagine you, of all people, having trouble with that."

Sam continued packing but didn't look up. "It's not that I can't do it. It's just getting old, you know? I can't even remember our address two moves ago."

His father smiled and said, "Mom found a great church for us to try when we went looking for a house on our last trip. Maybe you'll find some friends there."

"I sure hope so. We're leaving in a couple more days?"

"Yes."

Early on moving day, Sam woke but didn't feel well, kinda like he felt just before a big test, or when he had to try something for the first time, and everyone was watching to see if he might mess it up.

Still not fully alert, he stumbled toward the kitchen to grab something to eat before they left. After packing all those boxes, he felt like a bear that needed a long winter's nap.

The moving van had come the day before and hauled all their belongings away to who knows where. He wondered if he'd ever see his sports equipment again. *Those guys will probably see all that cool stuff and just keep it for their own kids*, he thought.

It would take two days for the Coopers to drive to their new home. Each member of the family had one suitcase with them. Everything else was on the moving truck. Again, Sam tried not to think about that too much. Besides, movers had gotten everything to each new house before, and he knew they'd probably make it this time too.

Though his father's work would be in the Everglades, the family would live in Harper's Inlet, north of Miami.

Not long after crossing the Georgia-Florida state line, Sam saw a sign for the Florida Welcome Center. "Hey, Dad, can we stop there? I'd like to get out and stretch a little."

His father half turned his head toward the back seat. "All right, but I want to keep on schedule."

The stop didn't take long, and the family began walking back toward their car when Sam spotted another family walking their dog in a grassy area not far away.

Sam turned to his mother, "Could I just run over and pet him for a minute?" Just because he didn't have a dog didn't mean he wouldn't want one.

"Yes, but make it quick," his father answered.

Sam darted over to where a medium sized, brown and white dog continued scratching in the grass.

"Is it okay if I pet him?"

"Her."

"Her?"

The woman holding onto the dog's leash nodded. "She's a girl, and she's very friendly."

Sam knelt down to pet the dog, but when he did, she jumped up, put her paws up to hold onto his shoulders, and proceeded to lick all over his face. He held up his hands, trying to protect his face, and she licked those too. "She sure is," he said between giggles. He pushed the dog away, got back to his feet, and ran back to where his parents stood.

"It's time to get back on the road," his father said.

"I gotta go wash my face and hands." Without waiting for permission, he dashed back to the building, rinsed his hands and then splashed water on his face. It felt funny when he used the power dryer on his face until most of the water was gone.

On his way out the restroom door, he noticed a rack of Florida attraction brochures near the far corner of the visitor reception area. *It'll just take a second*, Sam thought with a smile.

He had only picked out a couple of brochures when he saw a man standing farther over in the same corner with his back turned. It wasn't like Sam was trying to listen or anything. In fact, at first, he could hardly hear the man's voice at all.

Sam continued choosing brochures. He was especially interested in the ones that said "Everglades" or had swamp boat pictures on the front. *I've always wanted to ride in one of those.*

Then the man on the phone spoke louder. "Look, I told you I'd be there."

Sam stopped, looked up, and listened.

"Don't threaten me," the man demanded. "Are you threatening me?"

Sam gulped.

"Saturday, midnight, Harper's Inlet; of course I've got the date," the man said in almost a growl. "You're still running those boats with the sharks teeth and blood?"

Sam's mouth dropped open.

"Don't worry, I'll be there, and the boat had better be on time if you know what's good for you."

Without warning, the man ended his call and turned around. He and Sam were now staring straight at each other!

Sam dropped his fistful of brochures and sprinted out the door, down the sidewalk, and past his parents who were still standing near the car. He ran to his side of the car and called over his shoulder, "Come on, let's get outta here!"

CHAPTER 2

Interstate Terror

An hour or two later, Sam had fallen asleep. But that ended when he felt the car slowing down. While rubbing his eyes, he raised up to see that all traffic had stopped on the other side of the Interstate. Then he noticed what looked like dozens of police cars surrounding a small rental truck with their flashing lights still blazing.

"Accident?" Sam asked.

His father shook his head. "I don't think so."

As they moved closer to the commotion, Sam saw an officer holding back a large, black dog near the back of the truck. By now, traffic on both sides of the road had come to a stop.

"What's going on, Dad?"

"I'm not sure, but I'd say drugs."

"Drugs?" Sam asked. He could clearly see that everything that had been in the back of that truck was now stacked up in the grass. The dog sniffed and pawed at several of the largest boxes.

"This is about the only way drug traffickers can get from Florida to the cities up north, if they don't use boats or planes. The police call this 'the pipeline.' And they've named Interstate 95 'the drug corridor.'"

Right outside Sam's window stood a red, white, and blue Interstate 95 sign. That made him shudder. "How do you know about that?"

"In preparation for my new job, I had to take a course. They want us to make sure there isn't any suspicious activity in the Everglades. If we see something, we're supposed to report it."

Sam looked over toward the truck again as police officers lead away two men in handcuffs and placed them in the back of different patrol cars.

"What else did they teach you?"

"Well, most of the marijuana comes from Mexico. After they cross the border in Texas, they drive on Interstate 10, where we just came from. They drop off their drugs in small farm communities where others pick them up and then deliver them to Miami, or up north along the east coast.

Sam thought about that for a second. "But that truck's going the wrong way then."

His father shook his head. "They're probably carrying something much worse than marijuana."

"Like what?"

"Could be cocaine or other drugs."

"Then where do those come from?"

"Ships mostly. Big ships bring it in, in containers, and others drop theirs off onto smaller boats before they ever reach the harbors."

Right then Sam clearly saw the face of the man at the welcome center in his mind. As traffic began moving again, he slumped down as far as he could into the back seat so no one would see him.

Finally the Cooper family reached Harper's Inlet. Sam had never seen such beautiful, golden beaches, nor towering, coconut palm trees like the ones that swayed in the gentle ocean breeze.

The sea air also smelled different than back home. They had a clear view of the ocean from their front yard, even though their house wasn't actually on the beach.

The Coopers' new house looked different too. It had a rough texture on the outside. Most of the house was painted white, with light blue shutters and trim. Sam had a larger room than in his last house. But what he noticed most was how warm it was outside.

"Will it always be this hot?" he asked his mother as they ate sandwiches in the kitchen.

She smiled back at him and shook her head. "No. Down here, things are just the opposite from up north. We'll simply have to adjust."

Soon, Sunday morning arrived. It was time to try out that church Sam's parents had told him about. It was also time to see if he could make a few new friends. He tried not to dress up too much because he figured being the new guy would be enough to get him noticed. As they drove toward the new church, Sam asked, "Do you know anyone down here?"

"Just the people I'll work with," his father answered.

"Except for our realtor, I don't know a soul," his mother added.

"That makes us even," Sam said with a laugh, "except I don't even know the realtor."

He was happy to see the church parking lot almost full when they pulled in. *There should be a bunch of kids my age, with this many cars.*

Sam was taken to classroom eleven-B. He looked in and saw a sea of faces. Of all those children, he spotted a big, round face that stood out like an island in the middle of the Atlantic

Ocean. That boy had dark, nearly black hair, and he wore a bright Hawaiian shirt. It looked even brighter next to his tanned skin.

Against his better judgment, Sam headed for that big head and sat down.

First he took a deep breath, looked down and saw that the boy wore tennis shoes with no socks, and then said, "Hi. My name's Sam. Out at the front door, your mom told me to find you."

The large boy took a deep breath of his own, only he took a much longer time letting his back out. Then he turned to Sam. "Big deal. She tells all the new kids to come looking for me. Sometimes I really wish she wouldn't do that."

This isn't exactly a great start. Now what? he wondered. So he decided to sit there and mind his own business.

But the boy sitting on the other side of Tony leaned forward. "Hi, I'm Tyler. Nice to meet you, Sam."

Then another boy in the row directly behind them said, "Yeah, anyone who meets Tony automatically meets Erickson. He's Tony's shadow. They go everywhere together." Sam noticed that Tyler had a slight twitch as he blinked both of his eyes.

In every way that Tony was big, Tyler was not. He was skinny with spindly legs. His messy brown hair looked like a firecracker had gone off in it. His shirt was wrinkled and he held a ragged baseball cap in his lap. To Sam, it looked like no one took very good care of Tyler.

"I'm not a shadow," Tyler said. "I'm as solid as Tony is, just maybe not so big."

"Hey!" Tony said, and the class erupted in laughter.

"Children," the teacher said, "let's begin class now. Remember, last week I told you I'd have a new question for today. Well, this is it. Has anyone in the class done something you thought you had gotten away with, only to have someone find out about it later?"

No one raised a hand or said a word.

Sam considered for several moments: should he tell his story or not? If he did, then maybe the others would notice him and he might make some new friends.

That nervous feeling in his stomach suddenly got ten times worse. Then, for no good reason at all, he raised his hand.

"Yes?" the teacher said.

"I have." Sam could hardly believe he heard his own voice say that.

"I don't think I know you. Are you new to our class?"

Sam looked around to the others in the room. "Yes, I am."

"Would you like to tell the class a little about yourself?"

He squirmed in his chair at first. "Not really." Then he heard a few giggles from the others.

"Go ahead."

Slowly he began, "My name is Sam Cooper. I should be pretty good at this by now, because

I've never lived in the same place for more than two years."

"Well, tell us your story, Sam."

"You see, I love powdered doughnuts."

"The ones with that white sugar that just melts in your mouth?" a red-haired girl in the next row asked.

"Those are the ones."

"Man, I love those things," Tyler said.

"Anyway, they were in the kitchen, and my mom had given me three after supper. She told me that was all I could have until the next day, but I couldn't stand it. I really couldn't."

"So what'd you do?" Tyler asked.

"When I thought everyone was busy later that night, I sneaked into the kitchen, took down the bag, and started eating more doughnuts. I don't know how many I'd stuffed in my mouth when, without any warning at all, my dad came in the kitchen and turned on the light."

"No fair," a boy said.

"The thing is, I knew it was wrong, and I

knew I wasn't supposed to eat any more. Only I went ahead and made it even worse."

"What did you do?" the girl in front of Sam wanted to know.

"My dad asked, 'Are you eating *doughnuts*?' I held out my hands and asked, 'What doughnuts?'"

"What doughnuts," Tony snickered. "Classic."

"My dad told me to go look in the mirror. When I did, I saw powdered sugar smeared on my face. Then I looked down, and the stuff was all over my dark pants too." Then he smiled a little. "I guess you could say I got caught white-handed." He sat down, but when he did, he heard whispers all over the room.

The rest of the class period went by pretty fast. Sam wished he hadn't been the only one to tell a story about himself, and now he wondered if he was ever going to make any friends in this place.

At the end of the hour, their teacher

announced, "In one of our lessons coming up, I'm going to tell you the story of *The Stolen Watermelon*. You won't want to miss it."

"Sounds real exciting, I'm sure," Tony grumbled.

Before Sam could get to his feet, he was swarmed by the others in the class. They asked him all kinds of questions about where he used to live, what kind of school he'd be going to, and did he have any brothers or sisters.

Finally, Tony put his hand on Sam's shoulder and said, "You know, with a story like that, I think me and you might be able to do some stuff together. Give me your phone number. I'll call you up later this week."

Sam wrote his number on a slip of paper and handed it to him. "What kind of stuff?"

"My dad owns a marina. He rents boats and junk. There's a million things we could do."

"That's right," Tyler added. "Around here, people know that whenever Tony does something, anything, it's gonna be big . . .

really big. His birthday parties are the biggest, his house is the biggest, even *he's* big." Tyler stopped himself and added, "Big for his age, I mean."

"Hey, wait a minute," Tony protested.

"What's the matter?" Sam asked, "Too may doughnuts at your house too?" Then he laughed.

"You don't know the half of it, kid."

"Just remember," Tyler said as he held his arms open real wide, "if you get a call from Tony, it'll be for something big."

CHAPTER 3

Exciting Phone Call

Sam slipped silently into the seat next to his parents. But this time, in this church, he felt like things might be different. He'd already met more new kids in one hour than in a whole year at his last school.

"How'd it go?" his father whispered.

"Fine."

"*Fine* fine, or just fine?" his mother added.

"It was okay. I think I'm going to make good friends here," he whispered.

His parents just smiled back. Sam didn't think much of the preacher. That's not to say the man wasn't a good speaker. It's just that Sam had other things on his mind this morning.

He'd never had a friend like Tony before.

Make no mistake, he might have been a little too sure of himself at times, but Tony seemed like a good guy deep inside. Also it seemed to Sam like Tony could run the class if their teacher didn't show up.

Sam was already looking forward to that first phone call. In fact, right now it was all he could think about.

He was lost in his daydream, which lasted all the way through the sermon. He could tell because the next thing he knew, his mother poked him in the arm.

Sam was afraid he might miss Tony's call so he didn't go out of the house for the next three days. Still, when the phone rang, the call wasn't for him.

Every once in awhile he'd walk over, pick it up, punch the talk button, and listen to make sure it was still working. It always was. For one entire day, he even carried the phone around in his pocket.

Did I make a mistake when I wrote the number?

he wondered. Then he thought how funny it would be if he was off by just one digit. Tony could be calling the funeral home, the police department, or some other strange place. But that possibility only made him worry that he really might have written down a wrong number, since this was a new phone and everything.

What if I gave him my old number?

Thursday morning, the phone rang again. Sam raced to the den to pick it up, but his mother beat him to it in the kitchen. It really didn't matter, though, because the call was from some delivery place, so Sam hung up his phone.

I can't call him. Not only would that not be cool, I don't know his number anyway.

The following day, rather than spending the whole week like a prisoner under house arrest, Sam decided to ride down to the park on his bike.

He climbed a tree for about an hour, then

took a baseball and glove he'd brought along and played catch by himself. He'd gotten pretty good at that over the years.

After throwing the ball as high as he could and catching it for a while, he looked around for the tree with the fattest trunk. That turned out to be an old oak.

Sam took several steps back, and then began throwing the ball as hard as he could against that tree. Each time, the ball shot back toward him like it had been hit by a powerful batter. He'd scoop it up and pretend he was playing in the infield during game seven of the World Series.

Time after time, he imagined himself making the game-winning out in the bottom of the ninth.

After the fun and excitement, and the thrill of playing in yet another park had passed, he decided to peddle back home.

He slammed the back door and yelled, "Mom, I'm home."

"In the laundry room," she called back in a voice he could barely hear.

Sam walked in to see what she was doing, like it would be anything different than washing clothes. He was right, but this time she had her head in the dryer as she fished out a couple of his socks.

He breathed a long, heavy sigh and said, "I hate it when people say they're going to do something, and then they don't do it."

"Better be careful with that one. There's still the messy room you've promised and promised to deal with, and lots of boxes in the garage."

"I know, and I will, but Tony said he'd call me and—"

"That reminds me," she interrupted, "you had a phone call while you were out."

Sam's eyebrows popped straight up as his eyes widened. "I did? Who? When?"

"About an hour ago. I think it was that Tony. I left his number in the kitchen . . ."

Sam didn't wait to hear the details. He

dashed around the corner, down the hall, around another corner, and slid to a stop on the kitchen floor, right next to the counter.

There it was, a ragged little slip of paper Sam imagined was about to change his life forever. He picked it up in his trembling hand and just stared at the numbers. Now, after waiting all those days, he was almost too afraid to go to the phone.

When he finally got up the courage, it took him three tries before he punched in the right numbers.

I'm so excited. He took quick breaths as the phone began to ring. Then someone picked it up.

"It's your quarter," the voice said.

"What quarter?" Sam asked.

"Hey, who is this, and how did you get my private number?"

Now Sam wasn't sure if *his* mother had written down the right number. "Who's this?" he asked.

"You dialed the number. You mean you don't know who you were calling?"

Sam gulped. "Tony?"

"Lucky guess."

"Tony, is that you?"

"Hang on a minute, let me go take a look in the mirror."

Before he could say another word, Sam heard the receiver clunk down on a desk or something. Then, a few seconds later, he heard someone coming back. He picked the phone up again and said, "Yeah, it's me, who's this?"

"Sam . . . it's Sam."

"You're supposed to say, 'Tony, it's Sam, not *Sam*, it's Sam."

By now, Sam was almost dizzy. "Okay, okay. Tony, it's Sam."

"I knew it was you. Where you been? When I call, I expect people to be waiting to hear from me. Do you know how important this is?"

Sam almost felt like he had to apologize, as if he weren't allowed to have a life of his own.

"I . . . I went to the park for a few minutes. Anyway, my mom said you called."

"I did?"

Sam's heart nearly stopped beating. The silence that followed seemed like hours.

"Oh, right, I did call. You want to come over tomorrow and mess around? Tyler will be here too."

"I'm here right now," a voice called out in the background through the phone.

"Sure," Sam said, trying not to sound too anxious.

"Did I tell you my dad owns a marina and rents boats?" Tony asked.

"I think you did."

"Well then, did I tell you he also runs a scuba school?"

"I was just getting used to being out of school for the summer. What's a *scuba* school?"

"Are you serious?"

Sam laughed a little. "No, I'm Sam. Want me to go look in the mirror for you?"

"Okay, you got me. You know, scuba. Diving? Going under the water, but you can still breathe."

"Like the mask with a tube that sticks out of the water?"

"No," Tony scoffed. "That's snorkeling. Snorkeling is for sissies."

"But you do mean like with a mask and flippers?"

"Right, and a tank of air on your back."

"Really?" Sam felt like he might have just yelled into the phone. He took another deep breath before continuing. "I could never afford to pay for a school like that. It must cost hundreds of dollars."

"More than hundreds. The people have to buy all their equipment from my dad first."

"Well then, that's it, I'm out. There's no possible way. Besides, I've only snorkeled before."

"That's for sissies, remember? But you haven't heard the whole story. You're my friend, right?"

"Sure," Sam answered.

"My dad said me and two of my closest friends could learn for free."

"He did?" Now Sam was yelling again.

"Yeah, and Tyler is my closest friend. Well, he's always close, anyway. And then I thought about you."

Sam could hardly believe the words coming out of the phone. He had never made friends this fast before, and nowhere in the rest of the United States, not in all the places he had lived before, had he ever been friends with someone like Tony.

"Listen," Sam hesitated, "it sounds good. I really mean it."

"And?"

Sam thought he'd heard a disgusted voice on the other end. "Well, it's just that I'll have to ask my dad first, and I won't see him until tomorrow."

"*Tomorrow*? Hey, Sam, buddy, you can't let

an opportunity like this float past your window. There are plenty of other guys who would love to be having this conversation right now."

"That many guys would like to be talking with me?" Sam snickered.

"You know, there is something I like about you. Okay, tell you what. You call me back by tomorrow night. After that, I'll have to find a replacement. There's tons of guys who'd jump at the chance."

"Don't you dare. I'll call!"

"Okay then, boom," and he hung up the phone.

Boom, Sam thought. *Even the stuff Tony says is cool.*

Now how in the world was he going to wait all the way until Friday night before he could ask permission? Then he got an idea. He could ask his mom. If she said yes, then his dad would have to.

He ran to find her. It wasn't hard. She was still in the laundry room.

"Hey, Mom?"

"Hey, Sam."

"Do you know anything about scuba diving?"

She stopped folding the pile of towels in front of her. "You mean like under the water, with a scuba tank?"

"Just like that."

"I always thought that could be pretty dangerous."

This already wasn't going like Sam had planned. But he was used to the fact that anything new he wanted to try usually scared her at first.

"Yes," he said, "but people take lessons. They learn about the equipment, the dangers." He stopped and caught himself for a second. "Wait a minute; forget I said dangers."

His mother gave him one of those looks only a mother can give. "That's the problem. Divers get down there, under the water, where only fish can breathe. If they forget just one little thing, have an equipment problem, or run out of air, it's all over."

Sam felt his chest tighten. His chance of a lifetime was fading every time he said something. "I know, but what about if a guy was to study real hard, and learn everything?"

"Exactly what is it we're talking about here?"

Since his mother wasn't someone who could be easily fooled, Sam simply blurted it out. "Scuba diving."

"Scuba diving, and . . ."

"Me and scuba diving."

"Oh, I don't know, Sam. If I were the one deciding, the answer would be no right here and now, with no more discussion."

His shoulders lowered, and his lip quivered. "You're a hard one."

"When it comes to my one and only son, you can count on it. But you'll have to wait 'til your father comes home and see what he thinks."

Sam's shoulders made a slow rise back to normal. His mother hadn't said no, not yet anyway. "Thanks, Mom."

"There's still a chance," he kept quietly repeating to himself as he left the laundry room. But it would take at least sixteen hours until his dad would be back. And that was only if he came home on time. It might as well have been sixteen years.

I'm breathing and I'm under water, Sam thought....

CHAPTER 4

Scuba School Adventure

By the time Sam's father finally pulled into the driveway Friday evening, it was already getting dark.

When the pattern of the headlights from his car drifted across the wall in the den, Sam shot right out of his chair. He burst through the side door and arrived at the garage just as the car came to a stop.

"Hold it," his father cautioned. "I almost ran over you."

"I know," Sam said, short of breath, "but I couldn't help it."

"Are you that excited to see me?" his father said with a smile. "You know I don't bring you presents from these short trips."

"Not exactly."

"Oh, thanks, that really makes me feel important."

"No, it's not that. I'm glad to see you—it's just that there's something else."

"Well?"

"I met this kid in Sunday school, remember?"

"Tony, wasn't it?"

"That's him. He invited me to take scuba diving lessons with him and another guy."

His father put a hand up to his chin and stroked his short whiskers. "That costs a lot of money."

"I thought the same thing, only Tony's dad owns the school."

"Go on."

"He invited me to take lessons, and it won't cost me a thing."

His father laughed. "You mean it won't cost me."

"Oh, right. So, can I do it, Dad? Can I please?"

"What does your mother say?"

Sam's eyes sank toward the floor. "Can't you guess?"

"She probably thinks it's too dangerous."

"Boy, you really know each other, don't you."

"We should by now."

"She does think it'll be dangerous."

"It *is* dangerous."

One thing Sam's father knew about was how dangerous water could be. For most of his life, he'd worked around rivers, lakes, and oceans.

Since his father didn't say anything, Sam did. "So, can I?"

"We'll talk about it at dinner."

"Dinner? Have you looked at your watch? I ate over an hour ago."

"After I eat then."

Sam didn't intend for it to happen, but his voice turned to a whine. "Except I have to call him tonight or else."

"Or else, what?"

"Or else he's going to invite someone to take

my place."

"That doesn't sound like a very good friend to me."

"I'm the new guy, Dad, remember?"

"I see. I'll talk with your mother first then we'll tell you what we decide."

That wasn't exactly the answer Sam was looking for, but at least he hadn't heard the word *no* yet.

He decided to go to his room and wait for the verdict. He left the door half-way open. The wait felt a little like the TV programs his parents sometimes watched where you don't know what the jury's decision is until the very last minute. Now Sam understood what it must feel like, wondering if you're going to jail or not.

A full hour passed, and still no answer. *This has gone way past fun. Now it's heading straight toward torture.*

Just then, his bedroom door popped all the way open. His dad stuck his head in, and Sam tried to read the expression on his face. His dad wasn't a card player, but Sam always thought he'd be great at poker because you could never guess what was going on behind those eyes.

"Hi, Dad," he said with a sad voice. "No go, huh?"

His father folded his arms across his chest. "What makes you say that?"

Sam took a deep breath. "Nothing. It's just a feeling I have, that's all."

A broad smile came across his dad's face. "Well, your feeling is wrong. We talked it over, and I have just one question."

Sam leaped to his feet and jumped up and down. "What . . . what?"

"There will be adults there, teaching at all times, right?"

"Yes. They teach in small groups. I think ours will be Tony, Tyler, me of course, and maybe two or three others."

His father walked across the room and looked at a new poster Sam had just put up.

"And this only happens in a swimming pool? Not in the bay or the ocean, right?"

"That's right."

He turned back to Sam. "And it's all free, really free?"

"Totally."

"Then I don't see any problem."

Sam wasn't exactly sure what he just heard. It sounded like he could go. He quickly shook his head a couple of times. "Does that mean it's okay?"

"Sure, why not?" His father smiled before leaving the room.

"Thanks, Dad!" Sam called out after him. Then he hurried to the nearest phone. His hands shook again as he dialed the number, while his heart pounded like an Olympic swimmer who had just won the gold medal.

"It's your quarter," the voice said on the other end.

Sam laughed. "Did anyone ever tell you you're a nut?"

"Who is this?"

"Oh, no you don't. You know exactly who it is." There was a new confidence in Sam's voice this time.

"I guess you're calling me with the bad news," Tony answered. "Well, that's okay, I expected it. Like I said, there are plenty of guys who'd be dying to go. So I was about to call one of my other friends. He'll probably want to run over to your house and give you a great big hug."

"No thanks," Sam snickered. "But my dad said I can go!"

Sam heard Tony's phone drop onto something hard. When he picked it up again he said, "You can?"

"Sure. My parents both said it would be okay. So what do I need to do?"

"Just show up, that's all."

"Show up where?"

"You know where Dodds' Marina is?"

"You mean Dad's marina, don't you?"

"Are you making fun of my name?"

"Of course not," Sam said with a laugh. "I just thought Dodds' Marina was your dad's marina, dodd's all."

"You *are* making fun of me, and my whole family. I might just have to change my mind about this."

"Don't you dare," Sam threatened. "I was just kidding. Yes, I know where it is."

"Then ride your bike there tomorrow morning at nine o'clock. Bring swimming trunks and a towel. We have everything else."

"Even the water?" Sam joked.

"You're pushin' it, kid."

"Great. I'll see you at nine."

Sam hung up the phone. *How in the world am I going to get any sleep at all tonight?*

And he was right about that too. The ceiling in his bedroom had a tile pattern with lots of squares and diamonds. First he tried to sleep, but that was impossible. To make matters even worse, a bright moon lit up the night sky, and his bedroom. So he counted the squares on the ceiling.

This is too easy, he thought. *Those are so big.* Then he decided to count the diamonds. There were three times as many of them, and they made his eyes tired as he strained to count them all.

"Eighty-seven, eighty-eight, no, wait a minute, I did that one already, didn't I? Oh man, now I have to start all over again." But this time he only made it to fifty-five. At least that's the last one he could remember.

Wild dreams followed. In the first one, he dove to the bottom of the ocean to explore a shipwreck. Everything went well until he caught his air hose on a jagged piece of metal. It severed the line, and Sam couldn't breathe. When he woke up, his head was buried under both pillows.

The second dream was even worse. He found himself diving with his friends. Unfortunately, not long before he left for Florida, he'd watched one of the old *Jaws* movies on TV. So in his dream, he was suddenly being chased by a mammoth, man-eating, great white shark, and the shark's mouth was wide open. That dream nearly threw Sam out of his bed and onto the floor. The next thing he knew, his alarm woke him up. "Man, I'm glad that night's over."

Sam didn't waste a second. Even though he stumbled around at first, he still threw on his clothes, grabbed his swimming trunks from the doorknob, ran to the hall for a towel from the linen closet, and dashed to the kitchen for a quick breakfast.

"I want you to be careful," his mother reminded. "And don't eat too much. You'll be swimming soon."

"How many lessons are there?" his father asked.

Sam gobbled a slice of toast and gulped down a little orange juice. He swallowed, and then wiped his mouth. "Tony didn't tell me. I should know a lot more after today. Then I can tell you everything."

"Sounds good to me."

"I'm so excited, I can hardly breathe."

"I don't think you should go then," his mother complained. "The one thing you have to be able to do under the water is breathe."

"Not like that, Mom. It's just hard for me to calm down."

His father looked up from the newspaper. "You make sure to listen to every word your instructors tell you, and if there is anything you don't understand, I don't care how small it seems, you ask questions."

"Ask a thousand of them," his mother added.

"Don't worry, I'll be okay."

"Let me tell you something, son. When I was in the army, you know I was on a tank, right?"

Sam was already anxious to get to the marina and his great adventure. "I remember, and you never fought, and you only went to that shooting range and knocked down targets. You've told me a hundred times."

His father's look and tone grew more serious. "The point is, it was the guys who got it into their heads that they knew everything there was to know about their tank and weren't afraid of that beast anymore who got hurt, some of them real bad."

He raised his index finger and pointed it at Sam. "I want you to have fun, but as soon as you lose your fear of what can happen to you in the water, if things go wrong, that's when you can get into real trouble."

Sam looked down at the table. "I know."

"Promise me you'll remember it."

"I promise." Sam looked back up, hurriedly scooped the last of his breakfast into his mouth, slammed it down with juice, and asked, "Can I go now?"

"When will you be home?" his mother asked.

"There's a class in the morning, then we take a break for lunch. Tony said we can get it from some place in the marina. After that we have another class in the afternoon. That's all I know now."

"Do you have any money for lunch?"

"I think Tony's covering that."

His father took a few bills from his pocket and handed one across the table to Sam. "Here's a ten just in case."

"Thanks, Dad, but I really don't think I'll use it. He said everything was free." Sam hurried out the screen door, let it slam shut, and grabbed his bike.

"Oh no!" he yelled. "Not today!"

"What is it?"

"My front tire's flat!" He stomped his foot. "I can't believe this." Then he let his bike fall to the ground.

"Hang on a minute and I'll drive you down."

"Would you, Dad? Thanks."

Even though he left the house a little late because of all the questions from his parents, the car was faster than his bike would have been. At exactly nine they pulled into a circle drive in front of the Dodds' Marina sign.

"Just give me a call when you're ready to come home."

"I will. Thanks, Dad."

"And I'll take your tire in later today. In fact, your whole bike should be checked out anyway."

Sam ran toward the front door of the marina. Then he suddenly stopped. His father had almost driven back out to the street as Sam ran, waving his arms and screaming, "Dad, wait up, Dad!"

His father stopped the car as Sam ran to the window. "What is it?"

"Well, unless I want to be scuba diving in my birthday suit, you'd better hand me my trunks and towel." He had rolled them together, and his father picked up the bundle from the front seat.

"Here you go. Now be careful." He pointed his finger to the side of his head as he added, "And remember, think."

"I will. Bye, Dad."

Sam sprinted to the front doors and dashed inside, where he could smell chlorine from the pool. He also heard people yelling and splashing, so he followed those sounds.

As he came around the corner, he heard someone shout, "Hey, Powdered Doughnut, get your trunks on! Hurry up!" It was Tony, of course.

Tyler swam right next to him. "This is going to be so great," he said.

Sam found his way to the locker room, quickly changed, and then joined the others in the pool. At the same time, five men came into the pool area wearing special suits that said "instructor" across the front. They each carried four single air tanks to the side of the pool.

"Hey, you boys," one of them called out. "Get over here and help bring out the rest of the gear."

Tony said, a little too confidently, "I don't have to work around here."

"Look. I'm talking to someone who doesn't know how to scuba dive, and who won't get certified to dive if I don't teach him."

"Well, my dad—"

The man cut him off and snapped back, "I don't care *who* your dad is. In my pool you'll do what I tell you or you'll be outta here."

It looked to Sam like no one had ever talked to Tony like this before in his life. Tony thought about it for a moment. Then he said, "Sam, Tyler, you heard the man. Let's hop to it."

For the next ten minutes, the boys dragged out boxes of gear, more tanks, hoses, mouthpieces, masks, and flippers.

"I thought you said it was going to be fun," Tyler whined. "This is hard work."

"Yeah, well my dad's gonna hear about this," Tony fumed.

Over the next two hours, the class sat in a large circle as one instructor went over every piece of equipment. Then the other instructors made sure each person understood how everything worked.

"All right," the leader barked. "Time to suit up."

The boys helped each other slip on an air tank, tighten the straps, check the regulator, attach the air hose, and test the mouthpiece. That part hurt the inside of Sam's upper lip, but he wasn't about to complain.

Next, all the instructors stood at the edge of the pool with their backs to the water.

"This is how you enter the water," the main instructor announced. Each instructor held onto his mask with one hand, turned on his air with the other, and then, one by one, they simply jumped backwards into the water.

Next, it was time for the rest of the class to do the same. Sam felt a little nervous until he watched Tyler jump in. *If he can do it, I sure can,* he thought as he let himself fall backward.

When he hit the water, the weight of his body along with the air tank and weight belt pulled him under immediately.

He tried to hold his breath as he struggled to reach the surface again and get a breath of that wonderful air his lungs had come to love so much over the years. But, no matter how hard he fought, there was no way he was going to make it. *I'm going to drown in here, and nobody will see me.*

Then at the last instant, just before he thought he was going to turn blue and pass out, he took a breath. That sensation was such a shock, he began to laugh.

I'm breathing, and I'm under water, Sam thought, even though he had to clear a little liquid out of his mouth because of the underwater laughing.

He had never felt anything like this before. He knew right then he was going to like scuba diving a lot.

CHAPTER 5

Tony's Surprise

Sam wouldn't have minded if the lesson lasted all night and into the next day. Except, he had stayed in a pool too long once before and didn't want his skin to wrinkle up again like an old man.

After the lesson, Sam and Tyler helped Tony put away the diving equipment, then they sat by the side of the pool.

"So, Tyler, we know what Tony's dad does, and you know my dad is a biologist, what about your dad?"

Tyler turned his eyes down toward the water. In a voice nearly too low to hear clearly, he said, "We're divorced."

"You mean your parents are?"

He pushed his shoulders back and frowned. "What's the difference? When it happens, it breaks everyone apart. So, as far as I'm concerned, the whole family is divorced."

Sam stammered a little as he asked, "Who do you live with?"

"My mom and my sister."

"Does your dad live around here?"

"He moved to another town," Tyler said sadly. "But it isn't so bad; I get to see him every other weekend. Then on birthdays and holidays, they flip a coin. It's pretty hard sometimes."

"I'm sorry," Sam said, but as soon as the words left his mouth he wished he could have thought of something better to say. *Maybe that's the reason he sticks so close to Tony.* "So, Tony, same time, same place tomorrow?"

A broad smile came across his big face. "Indeed." It was clear Tony liked having the other guys look up to him.

"I have to call my dad and wait outside for

him to pick me up," Sam said.

Instantly, the old Tony was back. "What's the matter?" he asked, "Don't they trust you to go places on your own?"

"It's not that. I had a flat this morning."

"Flat head, flat foot, or what?"

"Flat tire, on my bike. My dad said he'd get it fixed while I was here."

Almost too quiet for anyone else to hear, Tyler said, "Sure wish my dad..." He didn't finish the thought out loud, but Sam clearly heard the first part.

Sam jumped to his feet, picking up his things. "Gotta go, guys. See you tomorrow."

First he went to the main desk and asked to use the phone to call home. Then he walked out to the parking lot. A few minutes later, his dad pulled up.

Sam liked the way he could count on him. If he said he'd do something, he did. This time, he brought the pickup, and sure enough, Sam's bike was in the back.

"Did they fix it?" he asked as he squeezed the tire.

Smiling, his dad said, "No, I like to carry around bikes with flat tires that nobody can ride."

"Thanks, Dad," Sam said with a returned smile as he climbed in.

"No problem; I just picked it up." He started the truck and drove away from Dodds' Marina. "How was your lesson?"

The same excitement he'd felt in the pool made Sam's words come more quickly and in a higher pitch. "It was the best. Have you ever gone diving like that?"

His father came to a stop, looked both ways, and then pulled out onto the street. "No, but I've always wanted to."

"It was the most amazing thing I've ever done when I wasn't dreaming. I mean, in dreams, a guy can fly and everything."

"Tell me what it was like."

"Well, it was kind of like one of those dreams.

I had all this stuff on, and they told us to jump in the water. You know how much I weigh, but I also had all these weights on and a heavy air tank."

"You probably dropped to the bottom like a rock," his father said with a laugh.

"Yeah, and the first thing you try to do is get to the top for a breath."

"But you had the air tank, didn't you?"

"Well, yeah, but right then you aren't thinking about it. I mean, you know that, but the part of my brain that controls breathing was not the least bit convinced."

"So what happened?"

"I tried like everything to get to the surface and take a breath. I thought I was going to die right there in the pool. So I fought and fought. Then, all of a sudden, I took a breath. Man, it was so weird."

"What was?"

"Breathing, just like the fish."

"Then what?"

"It felt kind of stupid, but I started laughing."

"Under the water?"

"It was the strangest thing. I almost choked. Well, I did, really."

His father became more concerned. "Did anyone come to help you?"

Sam shook his head. "I think that was part of the lesson. It was up to each diver to remember what to do, and then do it, I guess."

"But you could have drowned."

"Not really. There were instructors all over the pool. If a diver'd had any real trouble, I think one of those guys would have fished him out."

"How did your friends do?"

"They did okay, I guess. Must be they don't have the same dreams I do."

The truck came to a stop at a traffic light. Sam's father turned to him with a smile. "Lucky for them."

"I know." Sam looked over to his father. "Hey, wait a minute. What do you know about *my* dreams?"

The light turned green and they were on their way again. "Oh," his father continued, "in the last few years, I've only rescued you from, let's see, that burning building, the lions, and when you fell off the cliff. Those are the ones I can think of right now."

Sam shook his head. "I don't remember doing any of that."

"That and a whole lot more. Couldn't tell you how many times I've picked you up off the floor or untangled you from your blanket and sheets."

"Is there something wrong with me, Dad?"

"Because you dream like that?"

"Yes."

"No. It just means you have an active imagination, and that, I can tell you, is a good thing."

Riding back with his dad, Sam couldn't even imagine what it would be like without him in his life every day. He'd really never thought about that before, but now he understood, a little better, the pain Tyler must be feeling.

Sam didn't like how long his dad had to be away, but at least he knew his father would always come home again.

"Hey Dad," Sam said. His words came more slowly now. "Do we know anyone who's divorced?"

"As much as we've moved around, I don't think there is anyone you know. But your mom and I have known lots of them. Why?"

"Well, there's this guy Tyler. Today he told me his parents are divorced." He thought for a moment then added, "I could tell it made him feel really sad, even though he tried not to let on."

"Something like that can hurt a lot, that's for sure. Sometimes, it's the kids who think they did something wrong, or that they should have tried to help."

"How come you and Mom never did anything like that?"

"There isn't an easy answer to that one, Sam. It happens in a lot of families these days. The only thing I can tell you is, when Mom and I got married, we agreed that no matter how bad things got, and no matter who did what, divorce was never going to be a door we would ever open, not even a crack."

"Why not?"

"Because your mom and I believe when two people get married, it should be because they make a promise to love each other, no matter what. But more important than that, they've already made a commitment to love God as much as they can. If you do those things, then you look at life in a different way."

"I wonder if Tyler thinks he might have done something or said something that made his parents split up."

"That's not likely, son. I mean, there's usually been a lot of trouble between the parents before divorce finally happens. If you clear everything else away, most often you'll find one thing at the root of almost every divorce."

"Only one? What's that?"

"Selfishness—each person wanting what they want more than wanting anything else."

"I don't get it."

"It's still a little early for you to understand grown-up problems, but trust me on this one. Mom and I work at wanting the best for each other, not just ourselves. We've had some problems along the way, but we always work things out. You and I can talk more about it as you have questions and as you keep growing up into the fine young man you're turning out to be."

Sam leaned over and gave his dad a big hug. "I love you, Dad."

"I love you more."

Sam smiled, "I love you more than more."

"I love you more, times a hundred."

"I love you more than the whole universe." Sam stretched his arms out as wide as he could. When he did, his left arm hit his father on the shoulder.

"Okay, okay, you got me. I guess you love me the most, but I'll keep working on it," his dad told him. Just then they pulled into the driveway.

"I'll get my bike out of the back."

"Yes, you will."

Sam watched his father walk to the house. Somehow he saw him in a different way. Then he rolled his bike off the back of the truck and parked it in the back yard. When he went inside, dinner was cooking.

"Ummm, Mom, what are we having?"

"Since we live by the ocean now, I thought you'd like shrimp."

"Really? That's my favorite. And they don't even have to drive clear across the country to get it to my house now."

"I know. Why don't you wash your hands and set the table."

"Okay, but I've seen just about enough water for one day. I guess a little more won't hurt my hands." He headed toward the bathroom when the phone rang.

"Sam," his father called out, "it's for you."

He picked up the nearest phone, "Hello."

"Hey, you underwater breathing machine, what are you doing?"

"Tony?"

"You're not getting me on that one again. I know who I am."

"What d' you want?"

"Is your bike fixed yet?"

"Yeah," Sam said with a smile. "My dad had it with him."

"Well, then come on down to the marina. I have something great to show you."

"I can't."

"Are we going to go through that again where I threaten to find someone else, and you end up doing what I say anyway?"

"No, I really can't right now."

"How come?"

"We're getting ready to eat dinner."

"So what?"

"What do you mean, so what?"

"I mean, at our house everybody just eats when they feel like it."

"We don't."

"What do you guys do?"

"We sit at the table together and eat. You know, like a family."

"You mean all together at the same time?"

"Sure."

"With plates, and glasses, and forks, and spoons, and everything?"

"Well . . . yeah."

"Oh. Anyway, I just wanted to tell you Tyler was here. We've got something amazing to show you. Can you come?"

"No, I can't. And besides, we're having shrimp."

"Can't you just ditch your supper and get down here? You can eat shrimp around this place anytime you want. What I have to show you is special."

"I can probably do it after supper. Hang on, I'll ask." Sam rushed to his father and asked permission to go back to the marina.

"After dinner, of course," his father said.

"Oh, of course." He dashed back to the phone. "I'll be there in about an hour."

"An hour? You might be lucky if we're still waiting."

"You'd just better be, that's all."

"All right, see you later, Bike Boy."

Sam hung up the phone, washed his hands, and set the table. He liked sitting around the same table with his parents. It made him feel special, important, like he really mattered to his dad and mom.

At the same time, he knew what people said about Tony. When he called, it was going to be something big. *Wonder what it could be this time?*

"Tell me about your swimming," his mother said.

Sam was already working on his third shrimp. "Mom, it wasn't swimming."

"It wasn't? I thought you were in a pool. And didn't you take your swimming trunks?"

He nodded as he peeled shrimp number four. "I did."

"And that's not swimming?"

"If you're in the grocery store with food all around you, would you call that dinner?"

"It could be, eventually."

"Okay, bad example. We weren't just swimming. I was learning how to scuba dive, remember?"

"I know that, but how was it?"

"All I can tell you is it's now at the top of the list of the most fun things I have ever, ever done."

"Wow, that's saying a lot."

"It's just so different. I can't even begin to imagine what it will be like to dive in the real ocean."

"The what?"

Sam realized he hadn't told his parents about that part yet, so he chose his next words more carefully. "The ocean, Mom. Did you think people only went scuba diving in swimming pools? I mean, what would be the point of that?"

"Yes, but the *ocean*." She turned to her husband for support, but he didn't say anything.

"Water is water," Sam said. "If we learn what we need to know now, follow all the rules, and are careful, it shouldn't be any different. Plus, I get a certificate at the end and a license that proves I know what I'm doing."

"Sam, I'm not sure about this. I mean, there are whales and sharks in the ocean. "

He turned to his father to see if there was any help coming for his side, but his dad still didn't say anything.

Sam realized he was on his own with this one. "You're gonna have to let your little boy grow up one of these days, Mom."

"Sure I am, but I had always thought he'd grow up above the water, not under it."

Sam turned to his father again. "Can I go

ocean diving after I learn how, Dad?"

His father set down his fork and took a long, slow drink of ice water. "We can make that decision farther down the road. Right now, why don't you concentrate on learning how to dive as safely as possible."

Sam couldn't stop a big smile from spreading across his face. "My plan exactly."

Sam's all-time favorite part of dinner was always dessert, even on shrimp night. His mother made some of the sweetest pound cakes, puddings, pies, and other goodies anyone could imagine.

Tonight though, he concentrated on what the next big thing Tony had to show him might be. Finally, he couldn't ignore his thoughts any longer. "May I be excused?"

"But. . ." his mother protested, "I made something special for dessert."

"Tell me you didn't make that delicious chocolate pudding desert. With the baked crust, pecans, and the whip cream topping?"

She shook her head. "No, today I made something different. Since we live in Florida now, I baked a new kind of pound cake." She walked over to a cabinet. When she opened the door, she brought out something that looked fantastic.

"What's that?" he asked. His mouth watered.

She smiled at him, brought the cake over, and placed it in the center of the table. "It's an orange pound cake," she announced with pride.

"What's on the top?" Sam's father asked.

"I drizzled on a syrup I cooked with orange juice concentrate and sugar."

By now, Sam practically drooled. "You're killing me."

"I'm not the one trying to get out of the house."

"Could you hold it 'til I get back?"

"Sam, what do you think? Dad and I couldn't possibly eat the whole thing tonight, even if we tried."

"And if we did," his father added, "I think you'd be visiting us both in the hospital."

Sam took the longest time getting out of his chair. The whole time, he kept looking at that delicious, mouth-watering cake in the middle of the table. *This thing of Tony's had better be good.* "I'll try not to be long. It's just that Tony is so unpredictable."

"Well, be careful, that's all," his mother warned.

"I will, I promise." Sam said those words at the same time his hand hit the back door. He took a running jump as he pushed his bike down the driveway and hopped on. Soon he rode at top speed while his thoughts raced. *I wonder what it could be?*

CHAPTER 6

Watermelon Caper

Sam flew around the corner on his bike like Jeff Gordon crossing the finish line, five car lengths ahead of the nearest car in the Daytona 500. He stopped first at the front door, but it was locked. He looked at his watch, then he looked at the sign that gave the marina's hours. According to that sign, everyone had gone home almost an hour ago.

"Nuts," he said. *They must have gone on without me.*

Sam was about to leave when he heard a voice call out, "Hey, Bike Boy. Come on around back."

He pushed off in that direction until he saw Tony and Tyler next to something covered by a very large tarp.

"What is it?" he asked, as he coasted to a stop.

"A big whale someone caught today," Tony said.

"Really? Doesn't something like that start to smell pretty fast?"

"Don't let him kid you," Tyler said. He stepped closer to the tarp. "It isn't a whale. I've seen it already"

Sam scratched his head. "Then what?"

Tyler walked to the front of the tarp, grabbed a corner, and lifted it up so Sam could see part of what was underneath. When he leaned down to pull it up something fell out of Tyler's pocket.

"You still carrying that thing around with you?" Tony asked in an unkind voice.

Tyler straightened up. "Look, it's one of the only things I still have that belonged to my dad, all right?"

"Whadaya got?" Sam asked.

Tyler handed him a magnifying glass. It had scratches all over the glass, and some of the paint on the handle had worn off. "My grandfather gave his stamp collection to my dad and he gave it to me when he . . . you know. That thing came with it."

"Well, one of these days you're gonna be looking at something in the water, and that silly thing will fall right out of your pocket and wind up at the bottom of the sea."

Sam handed the magnifying glass back to Tyler. "I still don't know what's under the tarp," he said.

"It's a mini-sub, that's what," Tony said with pride.

"A mini what?"

"Sub. Submarine. It goes under the water and you can see stuff."

Sam whistled as he ran his hand along the sub's smooth surface. "Man! Can we ride in it?"

"My dad's going to have his mechanic check it out. After that, we all get to go out on the first voyage."

"Man, oh, man," Sam said as a feeling of total excitement took over his body. "And we don't even have to wear air tanks?"

"Nope," Tyler said. "It has its own air, but we take the tanks as a backup."

Tony pulled the tarp back down to cover the sub. Then he turned to Sam. "So how was dinner around the table tonight?" he mocked.

"Fine. It was fine."

"You guys eat at the table and everything?" Tyler asked.

"Sure. What do you do at your house?"

"Well, we eat together, but my mom's always watching one of those dumb game shows— the one where people try to figure out what the letters spell." He thought for a moment. "I'm not even sure we have a table. Oh, wait a minute, yeah we do. We just don't use it."

"What about at your house, Tony?" Sam asked.

He shook his head. "Nope. Never. I told you

before, I just eat whatever I want whenever I want. Who needs to eat together at a dumb old table?"

"Well, we do, okay?"

Tyler looked out toward the water. "You are *so* lucky."

Sam hadn't thought about it like that before. He was all caught up in another move to a new place. He had felt sorry for himself, having to be the new kid all the time. But now he was beginning to see what a good home he had.

Later that evening, his dad came in to tuck him in for the night. "Hey, Dad, did you know we're about the only people I know of who eat at a table together?"

His dad walked across the room and sat on the edge of Sam's bed. "We couldn't possibly be the only ones."

Sam propped up on one elbow. "We might be the only ones down here."

"Mom and I do lots of things for special reasons. That's because we only get one shot at being your parents and showing you what we think is important. Right now, you're one of the most important things in our lives."

Sam plopped back down on his pillow. "I know; I can tell. Thanks, Dad."

"Hey, you're worth it. Besides, you're pretty nice to be around too."

Sam smiled back.

"Got another diving class on Monday?"

"Yes." Sam rubbed his hands together and almost squealed. "I can't wait."

"Well, better get to sleep now. We've got church tomorrow." He walked toward the door. Then he turned and said, "Love you."

"I love you too, Dad." Then he yelled, "Night Mom! I love you!"

"You too! Good night!"

His dad turned off the lights, left the room, and closed the door. Then Sam started thinking, *I wonder what it's like at Tyler's house? And nobody seems to care where Tony is.* As he slowly fell asleep, he thought about his new friends.

On Sunday, a speaker came to Sam's church. Instead of their regular classrooms, all of the Sunday school classes met in one big room because a man with a guitar, and lots of puppets, gave a special program.

Monday morning couldn't come fast enough. There was so much to do. He wanted to hurry to the scuba class, but he knew his mother would make him eat breakfast first. As soon as he finished, Sam rushed to his bike and headed toward the marina. When he got there, he noticed workers had taken the tarp off of the submarine. Two men were already inside it, looking at the controls. When he didn't see Tony or Tyler, Sam decided he'd better hurry inside.

He quickly changed into his swimming trunks and joined the class just in time for the main instructor to blow his whistle and say, "Anyone who's late to one of my classes will sit by the pool and miss dive time."

Sam took a quick glance at the clock. *Whew!*

I still have a minute to go. He also decided he'd better come straight to class from now on. At a minute after the hour, two students came in, and they had to sit out the whole lesson. Sam could tell by the way they acted that they didn't like having to do that.

The class for today was called the buddy system. It was taught so divers would know what to do if their air tanks ever failed while they were deep under water.

The instructor had told them divers are never supposed to dive without a buddy. Right away, Sam picked Tyler. That meant Tony had to work with a guy who was at least twice his size.

For several minutes, the divers were instructed on how to take a breath, close their mouths, and pass the mouthpiece to the other diver. That person then grabbed the mouthpiece, pretended to take a deep breath, and then passed it back. Next they got to try it for real.

Once under the water, Tyler was the first to turn off his air, as if his tank wasn't working. Then he and Sam took turns breathing out of Sam's mouthpiece six times. Next it was time for Sam to turn off his air. The two practiced the same drill six more times.

After that lesson, Sam began to feel more confident that he could handle just about anything underwater. Anything, that is, except for a shark. *I hope I never look one of those monsters in the eye.*

Back on top, Tony stormed up to his friends. From the look on his face, Sam knew somebody was in trouble. "Hey guys," he blurted out, "thanks a lot for making me dive with Free Willy over there. I wouldn't mind sharing my mouthpiece with either one of you, but that guy? Whew!" He spit into the pool.

"If you're ever out in the deep and your air tank messes up, I don't think you'd be too choosy," Sam reminded him.

Tony spit again. "I think he ate a whole

garlic for breakfast!" He plugged his nose. "It was awful."

"Hey, you guys, let's go see the sub again," Tyler suggested.

The boys hurried to the back of the marina to see how the mechanic was doing.

Tony was the first to climb up the metal ladder leading to a hatch on top of the submarine. "What's it look like?" he asked.

"Looks like a sub to me," the man said without even glancing at him.

Sam had begun to notice that not many people seemed to like Tony much. He sure didn't have any friends around the marina. And Tyler only held on to him for security.

Some things about Tony bothered Sam. And he wasn't sure he could always trust what Tony said.

Each day after their diving class, the boys checked on the progress of preparing the submarine for its first dive.

"It shouldn't be too long 'til we can take her

out," Tony suggested.

"What do you mean, we?" one of the men asked.

Tony puffed out his chest. "Just that we get to go out in it, that's all."

"I never heard anything about that," another worker added as he chomped down on an unlit cigar in the corner of his mouth.

"Well, you guys might work for my dad, but that doesn't mean you know everything that goes on around here."

One of the men stopped turning the wrench he held and said, "Oh, and I suppose you do."

Tony let a deep breath escape through his nose. It made a long, loud hissing sound.

"Some of what we do know, you don't want to hear, Sonny."

Tony's face turned a dark shade of red. But Sam was pretty sure his friend wasn't embarrassed. It looked more like Tony was about to explode. He climbed off the ladder and walked back to Sam and Tyler. "I'll show those guys one of these days," he grumbled.

Trying to change the subject, Sam said, "I can't believe the week has gone by so fast. All this diving has been way too much fun. Thanks again, Tony."

"Yeah, thanks," Tyler added.

"It's all right," Tony sneered. "But there's a lot more fun stuff we could be doing."

"Well," Sam said, "I gotta go home. See you guys at church tomorrow?"

"Okay, see ya," Tyler said.

"Yeah, right," Tony said. "It's the high point of my week."

The next morning, Sam and his friends sat together in Sunday school again.

"Class," their teacher began, "do you remember what we've been studying?" No one raised a hand. "You should come prepared."

Tony fidgeted in his chair. "We go to school all the rest of the year. When summer comes, we get kind of prepared out," he answered.

Sam finally raised his hand.

"Yes?"

"Weren't you going to tell us a story about a stolen watermelon?"

"Yes. I'm glad someone remembers what we talked about before."

Tony sat up straight in his chair again. "He should; he knows all about taking food when he isn't supposed to."

The teacher began. "There was a boy about the same age as you children. He lived on a farm and on that farm—"

"He had a cow, E-I-E-I-O," someone said from the back of the class, and several of the children laughed.

"Okay, class," the teacher said, a smile pushing up the sides of her mouth. "On that farm there was no garden. But his place was next to another farm that had a beautiful garden. The farmer with that garden often won awards for the vegetables he grew. Some people even said there was something special about the rich, dark dirt in his garden."

The class got a little restless, so their teacher held up her hands for quiet before continuing. "Each year he would take his biggest, best watermelons to the county fair, and each year he returned home with many blue ribbons."

"Is that good?" a girl asked.

"It was very good. In the center of his garden stood a small hill he had made over the years. And at the very top of that hill sat the biggest, greenest, most shiny, watermelon anyone had ever seen. 'I'm going to win first prize for sure with that beauty,' the farmer said."

By now, most of the children leaned forward in their chairs to listen better. "Then what happened?" a boy asked.

"The farmer had always allowed the boy next door to eat whatever he wanted from the garden, all summer, except for the things he marked with bright yellow stakes pounded into the ground next to his most prized plants. The neighbor boy's favorite thing to eat in the whole garden was watermelon. But the farmer was so proud of his special watermelon at the top of that hill that he put more stakes all around it so no one could possibly make a mistake."

"Oh, oh," a girl warned, "I think I know what's going to happen."

"Then one day," the teacher continued, "the boy next door couldn't stand it any longer. When he saw the farmer and his wife drive away that afternoon, he sneaked into the garden, went to the top of that hill, and stole the melon. He couldn't possibly lift it, so he rolled it down the hill and behind a wood pile."

Sam noticed Tony had a sly grin on his face. "Classic. That's what I'd do," Tony whispered to him.

"The boy borrowed the farmer's handcart, quickly pushed the melon home, hid it behind a large brick barbecue his father had built, and ate the whole thing."

"Then what happened?" someone asked.

"Well, what do you do when you're eating a

red, juicy watermelon outside?"

This time several children in the class raised their hands. The teacher pointed to one of the boys behind Sam. "Yes?"

"We spit the seeds out right on the ground."

She nodded. "And that's exactly what this boy did. When he'd finished eating the melon, he buried the green part in the dirt, and covered up all the seeds. He figured that, by doing this, he had covered up what he had done."

"Pretty smart," Tony whispered again and nodded. "Too bad the kid doesn't live here."

"Well, when the farmer came back home, as usual, he went to check on his watermelon. As the date of the fair came closer, he did this several times per day.

"And that's when the boy heard him shouting for his wife. 'Ruth! Come quick. Something terrible has happened.' To make the farmer think he had nothing to do with it, the boy hurried over to see what had happened. When he ran into the garden, the farmer had sunk to his knees right on the spot where the melon used to grow. Large tears streamed down his face. 'Who would do such a thing?' he wailed.

"It sounded like the man had lost his best milk cow, not simply a melon. 'Probably some guys were driving down the road, saw your melon, and didn't know how special it was,' the boy said. 'We have people steal corn out of our field every year.'

"The farmer wiped his eyes and shook his head. 'I guess you're right,' he sighed. Then he pointed to the marks left in the dirt. 'At least it's good to know you would never do a thing like that.'"

"Guess he put one over on that farmer," Tony whispered. "So," he said out loud, "Is that it? He stole the melon, and covered up the evidence?"

"The boy thought that was it," his teacher said. "But he was in for a big surprise."

"Uh oh," one of the other boys said.

"For the next few weeks, the weather was

warm, with lots of welcome rain. The farmer and the boy's father were very happy for the excellent growing conditions. A few days after the weather cleared up, the boy's parents invited the farmer and his wife for a cookout at their farm.

"When the neighbor went to get his food from the grill, he noticed something behind the place where the meat was cooking. He set his plate on the table and walked around back for a closer look. He knelt down, and the boy watched as he pulled up something."

"I think someone's gonna be in trouble," Tyler said.

"'That's a funny place to grow watermelon,' the farmer said."

"'We don't grow any melons on our place,' his friend answered. 'That's because you've always been so generous with your crop every year.'

"'Then how can this be?' the farmer asked. He held a handful of young watermelon plants in his hand.

"Then everyone at the cookout turned to look at the boy. He had already begun to cry. Great big tears spilled freely onto the ground. 'I did it, I stole the watermelon. I couldn't help myself. It was so sweet, and tasted so good.' The boy was punished, and he had to help the neighbor in his garden for the rest of the summer."

"Man," Tony said, "talk about bad luck."

"It wasn't luck," their teacher corrected. "The boy *thought* he had hidden what he'd done: stealing. Sometimes those things are found out later."

Tony complained. "If I wanna do something bad, who's saying I shouldn't?"

Sam wondered what kind of bad thing Tony was thinking about doing. He didn't want to be part of anything he could get into serious trouble for. And he sure didn't want to think about trying to cover it up.

CHAPTER 7

Decisions, Decisions

When the family came back home, Sam found his father going over a few papers in his study before dinner. Sam was about to turn and leave. "Should I come back later, or is this an okay time to talk about something?"

His father put down his papers and removed his glasses. "I always have time for you; you know that."

"You know my new friends, Tony and Tyler?"

"Yes."

"Well, our lesson this morning was about how people try to cover up the wrong things they do, and how it still gets found out sometimes. What I was wondering about is

Tony said he didn't like to think about a God who would uncover what we do and let other people know about it."

"Then you have to be very careful around a person like that. Usually if you can't trust them in one area, you probably can't trust anything else they say."

Sam sat on the arm of the chair. "Well, I feel bad for Tyler because he hangs around Tony all the time, just soaking up whatever the guy tells him."

His father nodded. "I don't want you doing anything like that, Sam. I've spent too much time building trust and honesty between you and me. You're already old enough to be responsible for a lot of the things you do, and you know the difference between what's right and what isn't."

Sam scratched the arm of the chair with his fingers. "I know, but Tony is so much fun. I mean, he's got more money than anyone I've ever known before. It's so nice being around him sometimes."

"You mean Tony is your friend because of what he can buy for you?"

Sam sat up a little straighter. "Well . . . yeah, sort of."

"That's no kind of friendship."

"There's more to it than just that. Like I said, we get to do a lot of fun things together. Except for him being a little, well, dishonest, I like him a lot."

"Just be careful. I don't want you doing anything that could get you in trouble, or worse, something where you could get seriously hurt. Do you understand?"

Sam stood up to leave. "Sure I do. I'll be careful, Dad, I promise."

He left the den and went to his room to think about his friend and what his dad had said. Still, how could he turn his back on free diving lessons and all the equipment he'd ever need? And there was that mini-sub. It was painted dark red, and had big round windows.

Sam had already been able to sit inside of it once. He'd seen a place for the driver with all the controls and three seats for passengers.

He thought about the last time he'd talked with Tony. "My dad's gonna charge people for rides," he'd told Sam. "You, Tyler, and me get to take the first ride, right after our diving final."

At the dinner table that night, conversation was about the Everglades project.

"What have you found out so far?" Sam asked.

"I'm still gathering data. It's too early to decide how much of what's going on there is natural, and how much is because of what people are doing. I've still got a long way to go."

"Yeah, two years of work, hopefully going to five." Sam took a big bite from a hot, buttered roll.

"Right."

His mother passed the salad bowl. "Some ladies from the church stopped by today," she said. "They've invited me to be part of a group that meets once a week. It'll give me a chance to meet more people and make new friends myself."

"You need friends too, Mom?" Sam asked.

"Sure. Everyone does."

Sam took more salad and passed it to his father. "Hey Dad, did you know our scuba final exam is tomorrow?"

"No, have you been studying hard? Need any help cramming?"

"It isn't going to be that kind of test. We already did the written part."

"Well, what kind of test is it?" his mother asked. Her worried voice was back.

"It's pretty neat, really. You remember, Dad, when I was little—"

He smiled back. "You're still little."

"Yeah, well, littler, then. Before I knew how to swim, you took me into a pool and told me to sink or swim."

"I didn't really mean it though. I would have

helped you right away if you'd needed me."

"I know that now, and I know you were right there if I got in trouble. Anyway, that's sort of what our test will be tomorrow."

"How does it work?" his father asked.

"We line up on the side of the pool. The instructors put one air tank in each corner of the pool, and one in the center."

"Five tanks?" his mother asked. "Why do they do that?"

"We have to dive into the water without any air tanks on our backs. Then we swim to the first tank in the corner, turn on the air, take a few breaths, turn it off, and swim under water to the one in the center of the pool."

"Holding your breath?" his father asked.

"Yes. From the center, we have to swim all the way to the next tank in the far left corner."

"With no air?" his mother gasped. She put down her fork. "What if something goes wrong?"

"There's an instructor at each tank. And if

anything really bad happens, you just go to the surface and breathe. It's not that far to the top."

"It sounds a little dangerous," she added.

Sam shook his head and continued. He knew he was in the deep end right now, so he did his best to sound confident. "Well, from the corner we have to stay under water and swim to the one in the right corner. From there we go back to the center tank, and on to the one in the next corner.

"Then all we have to do is swim to the tank where we started, take one more breath from the hose, and we're done."

"That's it; that's the test?" his father asked.

His mother shuddered. "And everyone uses the same mouthpieces?"

"They'll be sitting in a pool of water the whole time, Mom."

"That's all there is to the diving test?" his father asked.

Sam nodded, but he didn't look back to his mother. He kept his eyes on his dad. "After we finish the test, Tony wants to take me and Tyler out in his dad's new submarine."

"Saaam!" his mother nearly shouted. "You never said anything about a submarine."

"It's better than the one at Ocean Adventure. It doesn't run around on tracks like a fish bus. This sub goes in the real ocean, with real rocks, real fish, and real seaweed."

His mother turned to his father. "What do you think about this?"

"We take our tanks inside, just in case," Sam told them. "What do you think, Dad?"

First he cleared his throat. Then a slight smile came to his face and his eyes seemed to twinkle. "I think if I had a chance like that when I was a boy, I would have done it, no matter what."

"You wouldn't have asked your parents first?" Sam asked.

He thought for a moment. "I'm not saying that, but I'd have found a way. As long as the sub has been checked out, and if you'll have

Tony's dad give me a call, we should be able to work it out."

"Man, thanks Dad. I can hardly wait."

That evening, Sam was in the den with his father. Since he was a scientist, he had a lot of questions when Tony's father called. But when the conversation was over, he told Sam it should be safe. Sam had to go to bed earlier than usual so he could rest up for his test in the morning.

Later that night, he had a couple more strange dreams. In one, everyone had taken their test. When it was his turn, he dove into the water and swam to the first tank. Well, he swam to where the first tank should have been, but when he got to the corner, the tank wasn't there. He held his breath as long as he could, then swam for the surface. Only, when he got there, he hit his head on a piece of glass covering the pool.

"I can't breathe!" he screamed. "I'm going to die!" When he woke from that awful dream he was all sweaty, and his sheet was completely wrapped around his head.

After untangling himself, he went back to sleep. In the next one, he and his friends floated around underwater in the sub. Without any warning, the scariest sea monsters he had ever seen in any dream slithered up to the big, round windows.

It was scary enough just seeing their frightening, furry faces up against the glass as they looked in on Sam and the others. Then, they began beating on the glass with rocks from the bottom of the sea. The monsters hit the glass so hard all of the windows broke at the same time. Water poured in so fast it was impossible for anyone to escape.

"We're all going to die down here," he cried.

When Sam awoke from this dream, he found himself on the floor, where so many other terrible dreams had ended, with the cup of water he'd put beside his bed poured all over his head.

Without any warning, the scariest sea monsters he had ever seen in any dream
slithered up to the big, round windows.

As he crawled up into bed again he sighed, "That's it. No more spicy food for me on the night before a big test."

When morning finally came, Sam felt like he'd been battling with someone or something all night long. *A guy shouldn't be this tired when he wakes up in the morning*, he thought as he yawned and stretched.

Since they were going to be in the pool early in the morning, the class had been instructed not to eat a big breakfast. They were told food would be served after everyone had taken the test, so Sam's mother made him some oven toast.

He liked the way she buttered it on one side, then tossed it in the oven on broil 'til that side was golden brown. The other side stayed soft and hot. While it was still hot, he quickly spread on a glob of peanut butter and squeezed honey on top of that. It made a gooey mess, but tasted so good.

Soon he hurried to his bike and was on his

way to the biggest test ever. *What if I don't pass?*
That'd be awful.

CHAPTER 8

The Ultimate Test

The marina was only minutes from his house. When he arrived at the pool, five tanks were already in position at the bottom. The main instructor held plastic discs in his hand with numbers stamped on them. He blew his whistle.

"Each of you will draw a number," he announced. Sam felt his heart beat a little faster. "This will determine your place in line for the test. Gather around and pick one. Remember, if you take your turn and can't make it, you go to the end of the line and try again. But be very careful. You only get two chances. If you fail, you have to take my whole class over again." Then he gave them a wry smile that wasn't very nice.

"I hope I don't get number one," Sam whispered to Tyler. When he reached out, his disc did have a one on it, but fortunately, it had a two after it. "Twelve," Sam sighed. "What a relief."

Tony drew number seven, and when Tyler pulled out his disc, his face turned the same color as the white caps of the waves on a stormy day.

First he gulped. "Anybody wanna trade?" he whimpered. Nobody did.

"Let's get lined up," the instructor barked. "We ain't got all day." He looked toward the group of swimmers. "Who's my first victim?"

"Me," Tyler said with a squeaky voice as he raised his number above his head. His eyes began their rapid, nervous blinking.

"Then let's get to it. You know what to do?"

Tyler nodded, but his hands shook. "I think so, sir."

"Think so? Under the water, you'd better

know so, Son."

He stood a little straighter. "Yes, sir."

The man turned and swept his arm out toward the pool. "Alright my boy, your ocean awaits you."

Tyler let out a deep breath. "Great."

He stood at the edge of the Olympic sized swimming pool and took several long, deep breaths so he could fill his lungs with as much precious air as possible. In an instant, he dove into the water and swam down toward the first tank.

From what Sam could see, it looked like his friend was able to make that one work without any trouble. Large air bubbles broke on the surface as Tyler swam to the center tank. That one went okay too.

But when he came to the one in the far, left corner, there were no air bubbles. Something went wrong. Then Tyler burst to the surface and took a deep breath, followed by severe choking. He struggled to the side of the pool and kept his head down.

Along with an instructor, Sam and Tony rushed over to help him out of the pool.

"What happened?" Sam asked, but Tyler didn't answer. *Tyler's a great swimmer*, Sam thought. *Now I'm worried.*

One by one, the other swimmers dove in and took the test. Tony didn't have any trouble. Then the next man after him had to give up with just one tank left. Like Tyler, he had to go to the back of the line.

After a few more divers had taken their turns, it was time for Sam to dive in. "Next!" the instructor barked.

As he stood on the edge of the pool, Sam's heart beat so hard he thought it might hurt the ears of the men waiting in the water. He took four long, deep breaths to squeeze in as much air as he possibly could. He breathed so hard it made a kind of whooping sound. But he tried not to think of what had happened to Tyler, or to the man who had also given up before finishing the test. He took one more breath and then plunged into the pool.

At first he couldn't see the number one tank. When he almost thought it was too late, he spotted it. Like a dolphin, he made his way in its direction as air began escaping from his nose.

I've got to make it, I just have to, he reminded himself. As fast as he could, Sam grabbed the hose, turned on the regulator, and with just seconds to go before he'd have to head for the surface, he took his first breath. Unlike the very first time, when it made him laugh, Sam was thankful there was air to breathe under the water. He took three or four more delicious breaths, then shut off the air and swam toward the middle of the pool.

Where is it . . . where . . . is . . . it? Got to be here someplace. There! Just fifteen or twenty feet ahead, he spotted the tank. As with the first one, he turned it on, put in the mouthpiece and began to breathe. He wondered what it would be like if he were really at the bottom of the ocean and his air tank didn't work. He imagined how it would feel to have to face death like that. But there was no time to waste.

There's the next one, Sam told himself, and swam to it a little more quickly than to the first tanks. By the time he returned to the center tank, he'd become more comfortable with what he had to do. His heart had calmed down, and he was able to think more clearly.

When he reached the final corner tank, he was almost sorry he couldn't continue. For many reasons, Sam really enjoyed scuba diving.

Finally, he burst to the surface in time to hear Tony yell, "Hey, you turtle head, what took you so long?"

Sam coughed a little as he swam to the edge of the pool. He looked up to Tyler. "Don't worry. You'll get your second chance. Just don't think about it much. Relax and have fun."

"Easy for you to say; you just passed." Tyler looked down at his feet.

"Well, I think you will too. You know all the steps. This time just do them when your turn comes."

The next several minutes seemed like waiting at a crossing for the longest freight train to pass by when you're trying to get to the ice cream shop on a hot day. But finally Tyler's second chance came. Again, he took his deep breaths, then slipped under the surface of the water toward tank number one. He handled it with no trouble, and moved to the center tank. Again, no problems. He continued until he was on his way to the final corner, the final tank, and the final leg of the test.

Suddenly, he began to come to the surface.

"Oh no, not again," Sam said.

But his friend quickly changed direction and, just as his feet kicked out of the water, kept his head under and dove back down toward the last tank and victory. Sam watched as the instructor made a note on his clipboard.

That can't be good, he thought. Finally Tyler

burst through the surface.

"I made it!" he yelled. He raised his fist into the air in true Olympic style.

The instructor looked at him for what seemed like forever to Sam, looked at his clipboard, then back to Tyler. "Next!" he barked again. Tyler had passed. Now all three boys could go diving. They collapsed onto a bench in the corner.

"I thought it was all over when you almost came up," Tony said.

"Me too," Tyler said softly.

"I wonder what it really looks like down there?" Sam asked.

"You were just down there," Tony said. "Did you have your eyes closed or something?"

"Not down there. I mean under the ocean."

"Oh, that. My dad says it's a whole different world. You can see all kinds of fish, some sunken boats, rocks, plants, stuff like that."

"Have you ever seen it?"

"Nah, but I hear the guys who rent from my

dad talking about what they've found."

"When do we get to go?" Tyler asked.

"We can ride in the sub this afternoon. It'll take some planning for a diving trip. You guys can come back around three."

Sam hurried home for lunch. A sense of calm, like just before a big storm, swept over him as he rode his bike along the street that was beginning to feel more like home.

He was glad he met these friends so soon. That had never happened before. He pulled into his driveway and parked his bike against a tree in the back yard.

When he walked in the house, his parents weren't home. That was okay because they hadn't planned on an exact time when he might finish his test and come home. But he was a little disappointed because he had such great news to tell them.

He decided to make a quick cheese and mustard sandwich. He topped it off with some chips and juice. Then he went back outside and ate on the front steps so he could look out at the ocean.

Just think of all the people who can only see the top of the water. The next words came out loud. "Now I'm one of the guys who can actually breathe under there."

He got so excited just thinking about the new world he was about to explore that he shook all over with excitement for a few seconds. That didn't happen often. Sam usually reserved that over-excited feeling for the biggest things in his life. And this was about to be a big one, he'd already decided.

Since no one came home by the time he'd finished his lunch, he left a note for his parents. "Sorry no one was here to celebrate with me, but I wanted you to know I passed the diving test. I'm now a real, live scuba diver. Yes, Mom, I said live. Tony and Tyler passed too. I'm leaving now to try out the sub. See you at supper, Sam."

He took a refrigerator magnet and stuck the

note in the middle of the door. That was the place where they always stuck most important family information.

Then he sailed out the back door, onto his bike, and off for his first submarine adventure. When he came to the back of the marina, a crane used for moving boats in and out of the water was just about to lower the sub into a spot right next to a wooden stairway going down from the dock.

"Come on aboard," the driver called.

Sam was the last to arrive. He parked his bike and joined Tony and Tyler as the three adventurers climbed into the little sub. Sam started thinking of all the underwater adventure programs he'd seen for years on TV.

As he looked around the inside of the sub, he could see where each section had been bolted together. The seats could hold two people. They were made of metal, painted black, and everything else was painted in a dark red color. But the boys each sat alone next to a window.

The operator sat in a single seat at the front. The lights in his controls were already on.

"I wonder if we'll see any treasure chests," Sam said.

"Not likely," the operator answered. "Probably a bunch of junk people have thrown away. I don't know why they think the ocean is a big dump. It makes me mad sometimes."

Sam wasn't exactly ready for a lesson on keeping the oceans of the world clean enough to drink out of. *Nobody can drink saltwater anyway, so why worry?* he thought.

The operator moved to the center of the sub, reached up, and pulled the hatch closed. Then he turned a big wheel that seemed to shut it even tighter.

"You might feel some pressure on your ears in a few minutes," he warned. "If it hurts, just plug your nose, close your mouth, and force air like you're trying to sneeze. That should clear your eardrums. You might have to do it a few times." He demonstrated it for them.

Sam looked out his window. There wasn't much to see yet, but since the glass was half in the water and half out, he could see a little over and under the water. Just then he was pretty sure a fish went by.

"Guys, did you see it?"

"See what?" Tony asked.

"That fish."

"You actually saw a fish?"

"Yeah, it was amazing."

Tony laughed. "That's about as amazing as finding a dog at the dog pound. I mean, what'd you expect to see in the water?"

Sam was beginning to see that sometimes it was better to just ignore Tony, so he did.

The motor of the sub started up while men outside untied the ropes. Sam had that nervous stomach feeling again. The boat bobbed up and down like the head of one of those fake dogs he'd occasionally seen in the back windows of cars. He wondered how the cheese and mustard were getting along in his stomach, which didn't exactly feel the greatest at that moment.

"Soon as we get under the water, we shouldn't be bobbing around like a note in a bottle," the operator joked.

And he was right. After he turned the small craft around, cleared the dock, and began to slip under the water, things became calmer. The ride was smoother and steadier.

That's when the show really began. Sam found it didn't matter where he looked, because in any direction, he saw wonders he'd only found in books before.

"Man, my ears are already killing me," Sam complained. He quickly did the "explode your head" air-blowing move the operator had shown them. Both of Sam's eardrums made a cracking sound, almost like setting off two firecrackers. Right away the pain was gone. "Hey, it worked."

"What worked?" Tony asked.

"I just popped my ears."

"Well, don't get any of it on me," Tony said

with a laugh.

"There is a lot of junk down here," Tyler said. "I see old rusty boat motors, tires, big oil-looking drums. Yuck!"

"You see anything good out your window, Tony?" Sam asked.

"Nothing other than the fish and garbage, but I'll let you deep sea explorers know if I do."

The water near the docks was a little cloudy. It made it hard to see things clearly. As they headed out farther, the water became a little clearer.

"This is better than a little pretend ride at Ocean Side Park. They don't even float," Tony said with a laugh.

"I know," Tyler added. "Don't see any tracks down here either."

After about half an hour, the operator announced, "Time to turn 'er around and head back in to dry land, guys."

"Oh, can we stay out just a few more minutes, please?" Tyler begged.

"Nope. She's almost out of fuel. I need to top off the tanks. This was just a quick test to see if all the systems worked. They do, so it's in we go."

"No fair," Sam complained. He pretended to be angry by stomping his feet.

"There'll be other times."

"Don't forget, you guys. Now we can do some real diving on our own," Tony reminded them.

"When can we do that?" Tyler pleaded.

"Let's talk about it when we get back to the dock."

That seemed a little odd to Sam. Suddenly Tony became secretive and quiet. Sam wondered if he didn't want the man running the submarine to hear him.

In a few minutes, they arrived back beside the dock. Slowly, the boat came to the surface as it coasted the last twenty or thirty feet to a stop. A harness was attached again, and the sub was gently lifted out of the water onto a special place designed for it when it wasn't taking passengers for rides.

The operator once again walked to the center of the boat and turned the big wheel. Then Sam watched as the hatch popped open. The sun came in, but so did water that had gathered on the top. With a feeling of sadness, he followed his friends up the ladder and out onto the dock.

"Let's go someplace where we can talk." Tony continued in his mysterious sounding voice.

They found a place over by the gas pumps and piles of ropes.

"These remind me of scary snakes that live in the ocean," Tyler said.

"No kidding," Sam added. "I saw this program once where these divers swam around next to a bunch of rocks. Then, all of a sudden, these creepy, black, snake-like things jumped out at them. Man, that scared me so bad."

"I hope we don't see anything like that where we're going," Tyler whined.

"So what's the big mystery?" Sam asked.

Tony looked at them thoughtfully for a moment. "We're going out for our first solo dive tomorrow."

"Really?" Sam asked.

"Really."

"Is your dad going to call my dad like before?"

"Not this time. I've already got it set up."

"I don't think my parents are going to like that."

"My mom won't care," Tyler said. "She's too busy to care about much of the stuff I do anyway."

"Man, I don't know," Sam hesitated.

"What's the matter?" Tony asked in one of his familiar tones. "Don't you trust me?"

Sam didn't say a word. He couldn't stand the thought of being left on the dock and missing all the fun. "I'll have to see," he said. "Why can't your dad call?"

"Cause he's out of town on a buying trip.

He won't be back for three days. You wanna sit around and think about it for three whole days?"

Sam looked out across the water and shook his head. "No, I guess not."

"Then it's a deal. Tomorrow we go out where the real adventures are."

Suddenly the sun disappeared and the boys felt raindrops, so they ran inside the marina. One of the things Sam liked about Florida was the way the storms blew up. It could be sunny and warm one minute and then all of a sudden the wind would pick up, the sky would turn dark, and a tremendous rain would drench anyone unfortunate enough to be caught outside.

He liked to watch a good rain. The air smelled like fish, and the raindrops seemed to wipe everything clean.

Once, when he was riding with his dad, a storm just like this blew in. He remembered seeing a man with white hair trying to close the top of his older convertible, only the wind was so strong, he had trouble getting the cloth top down. The man had gotten very wet.

Right now, the wind blew so hard the rain looked like it was falling sideways. He looked out toward the ocean in time to see a huge bolt of lightning, followed by a gigantic boom.

"That sounded pretty close," Tyler said.

"Know the way you can tell how close?" Sam asked.

Tyler shook his head. "Huh-uh, how?"

"Well, as soon as you see the flash, you count, one thousand one, one thousand two."

"Why do you do that?"

"Each time you count like that, it takes about a second. And each second counts for a mile. So from the flash to the boom, the seconds tell you how many miles away it is." Just then, there was a tremendous flash, followed immediately by a boom that shook the marina.

"I never got to count," Tyler complained.

"I know," Sam said as he looked around.

"That one *was* close."

Tony waved his hand toward Sam. "Aw, that's nothin'. Everybody knows how to do that."

"I didn't," Tyler said.

"Just remember, you guys," Tony said, "thunder might make the noise, but the lightning does all the damage."

Sam looked toward the ocean again and shuddered. "I'd sure hate to be the guy who's stuck out there in this storm." He shook his head. "Man, that'd be awful."

CHAPTER 9

Sailing at Sunrise

The storm finally let up, the sky cleared again, and the sun came out. Sam went outside, shook the water droplets off of his bike, wiped the seat with his shirt, and started toward home.

He didn't know how, but he had to find a way to get permission so he could go on the diving trip. He didn't want the other guys to think he was afraid, or that he always had to do what his parents told him.

At dinner he didn't eat much. In his mind a fierce battle raged. Then he remembered the cartoons he'd seen where a guy is trying to make the right decision. On one shoulder perched an angel with a halo over its head, and on the other shoulder sat, well, the other guy.

"Sam, Sam, my boy. What's the big deal?" the bad one seemed to say. "All's you gotta do is tell them a little white lie. Nobody needs to know but you."

"Oh, no, sweet Samuel. Remember, your name comes from the Bible. How could you even think of telling a lie?"

"Aw, buzz off you goodie-goodie," the first character said.

The good one stood to his feet. "But you must tell the truth. Remember those doughnuts?"

"Yeah, remember how sweet and delicious they tasted? It was worth it. Too bad you didn't get out of the kitchen in time, little buddy."

The good one folded his arms and turned his head away from Sam. "Don't listen to him, Sam."

"But Sammy, just think of all the fun you'll be missing if you tell the truth. And those guys'll just think you're chicken."

The other character turned back to Sam.

"Parents always seem to find out when you do something you shouldn't."

Trying to change the subject, the first one quickly said, "That Tony. He's quite a guy, don't you think?"

"Tell the truth, Sam, and you'll never be sorry."

"Sorry? Sorry? That's one of the sorriest things you've said as long as we've been working together."

"It's true. Telling the truth makes life much easier."

"Who wants easy? We're talking about fun here, serious fun. Have you forgotten already, Sam, my boy?"

"Sam," his father's voice broke in, "*what* are you doing?"

His father's voice jolted Sam back to reality. He looked down to see he had been scooping up his mashed potatoes with a spoon and mixing them in his glass of milk.

"Is that some kind of new milkshake?" his

mother said with a laugh.

Sam shook his head and blinked a couple of times. "Oh, no. Sorry. I was just thinking about something."

"I'll say. So what is it?" his father asked.

"Well, you know Tony?"

"Yes, of course we do."

"And you know we just finished our diving class and that submarine trip."

"Right."

"Well, now we want to go out and dive in the real ocean."

His mother leaned into the table. "And there'll be adults with you?"

Sam shook his head. "Um, no. Just us guys."

"Does Tony's dad know about your plans?"

"Tony says he does."

"Will he be calling me again with the details?"

"Not this time. He's on a trip someplace."

"Then the answer is no," his father said.

Sam didn't mean to argue, but he was about

to see his diving adventure disappear, just like the thunderstorm earlier. Now his voice sounded defensive. "Oh, Dad, come on. You're always telling me to be careful, and to try new things at the same time. I'm confused."

His father smiled slightly. "You'll make a great lawyer one day."

Sam smiled back. "Then I can go?"

His father held up both hands. "Not so fast. If you want to wait until I can go out with you some other time, you can dive all day if you want to. But there'll have to be adults with you who know what to do."

"This is so not fair, and you don't even know how to dive," Sam grumbled as he pushed himself away from the table.

"I didn't hear anyone say you were excused," his father told him.

Sam slumped down again into his chair. The corners of his mouth curled straight down. "May I be excused...*please*?"

"Yes."

Sam let out a blast of air from his lungs, placed both hands flat on the table, and stood up. He plodded toward the hallway, walking so slow, it seemed like he was in a funeral march. When he reached his room, he had an idea. Quickly he dialed Tony's number.

"It's your quarter," the familiar voice answered.

Sam liked it that Tony had his own, private line. That way he didn't have to talk to his parents. "Hey, Tony. What time are you leaving tomorrow?"

"Six a.m. At six-o-one you'll be too late. Did your dad say you could go?"

"Not exactly. Why?" Sam nearly said with a whisper.

"But you're still going, right?"

First Sam gulped. Then he said, "I'll see you at six."

"Alright. Boom!"

After Tony hung up, Sam had a bad feeling. He knew he was about to do something wrong—really wrong. And he knew he would be in big trouble after he got back, probably the biggest trouble of his entire life. But he'd already decided. He was going.

That night he had another series of terrible dreams. In every one, he found himself doing something he shouldn't, getting caught, and then being punished for it. He even dreamed he was the boy who stole the prized watermelon from the farmer. But in this dream the seeds grew like Jack's beanstalk, into a powerful plant that grabbed him by the ankles. When he fell to the ground, that monstrous vine quickly pinned him down by his arms, around his neck, and body. "Help, somebody help, please!" Sam cried out.

After this dream, he woke up half on and half off his bed. He found himself wrapped up in his blanket like a mummy. *I should just start out sleeping on the floor. It'd be so much easier.*

As he climbed back in bed, he hoped the triple-feature at the dream theatre multiplex was over, but it wasn't.

Sam hadn't read the book nor seen the cartoon for a few years, but the next dream was all about Pinocchio. In this dream, Sam *was* Pinocchio. *Pinocchio*? he wondered. *Wha . . . what's this*?

He sat on the shelf in his dad's workshop. His father was just finishing a few final touch-ups of some of his paint. The next thing he knew, Pinocchio-Sam began telling lies so fast, his nose started growing. It didn't just grow a little. The crazy thing grew like a redwood. Birds made nests in it. His nose got so heavy, Sam couldn't hold his head up any longer. So he took a crutch from the workshop and propped his nose up on that.

When he looked out, he noticed a few boys in ragged clothes coming near. "Who are you?" Sam asked.

"We live on this island you've come to. How did you get here?"

Sam tried to shake his head but the long nose

made that impossible. "I don't know. What's the name of your island?"

"It's the Island of Lost Boys," one of them said with the saddest voice, even sadder than Tyler's.

"I don't think I like the sound of that." Sam struggled to get up, but his huge, long nose held him down. The boys gathered around him and bellowed the most evil laughter he had ever heard.

"Let me up. Let me up," Sam cried. "I can't breathe."

When he woke up again, he saw he'd been lying flat on his chest with his face buried in the pillow. He slowly rolled over onto his back and said, "I hope this trip is gonna be better than doughnuts."

After that, it was impossible to go back to sleep. Not because he wasn't tired; he sure was. But Sam didn't think he could take one more scary dream. He'd had enough to last him for months.

At five-thirty, he slipped out of his covers, dressed quickly, grabbed his swimming trunks, and crept down the hall.

In the kitchen, he stopped to write a quick note. "Gone to see Tony and Tyler. Be back for supper." Even after he wrote the last words and set the pencil down, he knew it wasn't the truth.

Safely outside, he grabbed his bike and raced toward the marina. The early morning air was cool and damp. A light mist surrounded him as he rode, and his bicycle seat was wet. *Wish I'd had time to dry it off.*

Sam had never been to the marina so early. The sun wasn't up yet so only a few lights cut through the darkness. Just going there didn't feel right. *Too late now,* Sam thought.

When he coasted around back, he found his two friends already there, getting ready. Tyler carried a box of food, while Tony finished loading the last two air tanks onto a boat he'd tied at the dock.

"Hey, didn't think you were gonna make it," Tony mocked.

"Well, I did," Sam said with a sense of pride.

"How'd you get past your parents?"

"None of your business, okay?"

Tony tilted his head from one side to the other. "Somebody might be sneaking off without telling mommy and daddy," he teased.

Sam parked his bike in the rack. When he took a closer look at the boat his friends were loading, he noticed something.

"Hey, what kind of boat is this anyway?"

"It's a catamaran," Tony said.

"A cat-a-ma-what?"

"Catamaran. Haven't you ever heard of a catamaran?"

"Don't forget," Tyler joked, "he's an inlander."

"We had lakes where I came from, but that thing looks like two boats with boards across the middle."

"That's what a catamaran is, really. See,

a regular sailboat goes down real deep in the water. Look over there at that one." Tony pointed to another section of the dock.

Sam turned to see a boat having some work done on the bottom. It had been lifted clear out of the water and set in a large rack.

Tony continued. "A regular sailboat has to have about as much sticking down into the water as it has sticking out."

"How come?"

"Because when Mr. Wind comes along— and he can blow real hard sometimes— the boat would flop right over if it didn't go down deep."

"I think I get it, but why won't a cat-a . . . cat-a . . ."

"Catamaran."

"Right. Won't it fall over too?"

"It's like the difference between a motorcycle and a car. The motorcycle only has two wheels. If it decides to lay down on a sharp curve and die, it does. But a car has four wheels. It takes a lot more to tip it over."

"I get it."

"The sailboat goes down deep, but the catamaran kind of skims along on the surface. It's a lot faster. It'd take a pretty bad storm to turn this baby over."

"Do you know how to sail it?"

"Do I know how to sail it? Hey Tyler, do I know how to sail a catamaran?"

Tyler looked up from where he was arranging a rope and laughed. "He was practically born on one."

"Is it okay with your dad if we take it out?" Sam asked.

Tony didn't exactly answer the question. "He rents these jobs to people who know a lot less than I do. Sure, it's okay. Don't worry."

Sam tried to ignore the answer. If he were looking for an excuse not to go, Tony had given him a whopper.

The sun began to rise higher in the sky. Colors of blue and black gave way to oranges and reds. The air felt completely still.

"Hey, Tony," Sam asked, "this is a sailboat too, isn't it?"

"Sure, why?"

"Well, doesn't it need wind to sail?"

"You really don't know anything, do you?" Tyler said.

"What's that mean?"

Tony cleared his throat and spit in the water. "It has a small motor on the back. We use that to get out of the harbor. When we go out on the open water, the wind will start whipping up. Don't you worry about it, you'll see."

"Whatever you say," Sam sighed.

"Sam," Tony said, "before we leave, why don't you stick your bike around behind the shed." He pointed to a small building off to the side.

"Why?"

"Just do it," Tony ordered.

It seemed like a strange request. Sam had always parked his bike in the same rack every time he'd come to the marina. And he'd also noticed no one went into the shed very often. But Tony was in charge, and whatever Tony said, people usually did.

When he came back, Tony gave another order, "Untie the ropes so we can get this trip started."

Sam did as he was instructed, and the boat floated away from the dock. "Hey, wait for me," Sam yelled.

"Be quiet, and jump," Tony grunted through a whisper.

With only inches to spare, Sam leaped onto the boat. He hit with such force, it made him roll like a rugby player. If the railing hadn't been there, he would have dropped off the other side and plunked right into the drink. "That was a close one," he said as he got back to his feet.

Tony started the motor, and they made their way toward the larger opening of the small port. Sam noticed Tony had been right about the wind. He could already feel it picking up as gusts occasionally blew his hair into his eyes.

It wasn't long before they passed the long pier that ran way out into the ocean. It was made of wood and sat high out of the water up on stilts. This pier even had small buildings on it.

Like a seasoned sailor, Tony began barking orders. "Let's get this tarp off the sail so I can hoist it up the mast."

None of this made a bit of sense to Sam, so he watched what Tyler did and tried his best to copy him. In minutes, Tony pulled on a rope while the beautiful sky-blue sail rose into the air like a proud flag.

The wind quickly found it and filled the sail. It looked like half of a hot-air balloon to Sam.

The boys had often gone to Tony's house because he had the biggest flat-screen TV in town. One of their favorite programs to watch on that monstrosity was reruns of Gilligan's Island. Tyler started singing the theme song.

The others joined in and sang together, "A three hour tour, a three hour tour." Then they laughed.

At that moment, Sam forgot about the lie he'd written. In fact, he forgot about everything except the wind, the sea, and this great boat which was already skimming across the choppy water at what felt like high speed to Sam. "Where are we going, exactly?" he asked.

"Exactly? Couldn't tell you exactly," Tony answered. "But I'm taking us out to an area where a lot of the renters go to dive."

"Did you say die?"

"Dive. I said dive. There's supposed to be some old wrecks out there."

"Ships?"

"Well, cars sure can't drive out here," Tony said with a laugh.

"Can I steer the boat, Tony?" Sam asked.

He laughed and said, "In your dreams."

Sam thought for a moment, remembered the night he'd just had, and sighed, "I sure wish you hadn't said that."

"Said what?"

Sam looked out over the vast ocean. The beach faded farther and farther into the distance behind them. "Never mind."

CHAPTER 10

Deadly Storm

By the time the morning sun hung high in the sky, Tony said, "That's strange."

"What? What's strange?" Tyler asked.

"Have you guys seen any other boats out here?"

"No," Tyler answered in his patented, panicked voice.

"Me neither," Sam added as he scanned the horizon.

"We've been out here for almost two hours, and I haven't seen a thing. We should be about fifteen minutes away from the best diving spot in the whole, wide world, and I don't see a single boat anywhere." Tony picked up a pair of binoculars and continued his search. He panned back and forth over the water.

"There was that tanker, remember?" Tyler asked.

"Yeah, but I mean small stuff like us. Lost Island is about five miles from here, if I remember right."

"Lost Island?" Sam asked.

"It isn't really lost, Sam. They just call it that. I mean, there's another one called Pelican Island. You don't think it looks like Big Bird, do you?"

"I think it's because so many boats have been lost on the rocks out there," Tyler said.

A few minutes later, Tony began pulling down the main sail. That slowed their boat. "Get your tanks ready. We're right on top of our dive zone."

Tyler handed one of the air tanks to Sam. "Tanks a lot," Sam joked. It only took a few minutes before the boys had all of their gear on and were ready to fall backwards into the water.

"On three," Tony announced. "Make sure you have your air turned on." Then he counted out and raised his index finger each time, "One . . . two . . ."

Sam's heartbeat quickened. Was he really getting ready to do this?

"Three!"

Together, the young divers made one big splash into the ocean, quickly turned over, and swam down toward the bottom. The area Tony had picked was clear and not too deep.

If Sam had thought the submarine ride was exciting, it was nothing like being completely on his own under the water. He wondered if this was what it felt like to a new pilot who finally flew alone for the first time. Next, he thought about the day he would be able to drive a car all by himself. Then he decided he'd better concentrate on this dive.

Sam could hardly believe it when he looked at the expensive diving watch Tony had loaned him. Thirty minutes had gone by like they were thirty seconds. He'd learned in class that a diver needs to keep an eye on the time so he knows when his tank is about empty. Tony didn't want to be bothered with that, so he'd given the duty to Sam.

Sam got the attention of the other two and began pointing, first to the watch, and then toward the surface. At first Tony and Tyler just shook their heads, because they had been looking at something on the bottom. But with his rapid movements, Sam insisted it was time. Since he was the designated watch watcher, the others had to obey.

Back on the boat, Tony looked toward the sky. He was usually pretty brave. At least he acted that way, but Sam noticed a slight look of fear on his friend's face.

"Get your equipment off and put it away," Tony ordered after removing his tank. The boys quickly slipped their clothes on over their swimming suits. Then Tony hurried to raise the main sail. When he did that, the already strong wind pushed their small boat until it was traveling like a NASCAR racer across the water.

"Anything the matter?" Sam yelled over the sounds of the wind and the waves.

"I don't like the color of that sky over there," Tony said. "And we're going the wrong direction. Here, Tyler. Take the wheel and get us turned around. I'm gonna check with the Coast Guard on the radio."

Tyler grabbed the controls while Tony went into the small cabin between the two boat parts of the catamaran. Since Sam didn't have a job to do, he went with Tony. His friend switched on the small radio and punched in a number. What Sam heard next made his hands turn cold and sent a chill straight up his back.

"Repeat," a voice crackled over the radio, "a small craft warning is in effect. This is a serious storm. The National Weather Service is reporting that this storm formed rapidly and has intensified in the last two hours. It may be upgraded to a tropical storm."

Tony sat like a stone and continued listening. "I never heard anything about bad weather."

It was like one of Sam's terrible dreams. Only, this time the dream was real. "Your dad rents boats. Didn't you check the weather report before we left?"

Tony only shook his head.

The two continued listening to the radio. "If you are out on the water, return to port immediately. Repeat, return to port immediately. You don't have much time."

Tony scurried back outside to take another look at the sky.

"I don't like the looks of those clouds," Tyler warned. "I've been watching, and they just came up out of nowhere. I'm really scared, Tony."

As Sam scanned the black clouds in the stormy sky, there were frequent bolts of blinding lighting so fierce they seemed to split the ocean wide open when they hit. And the thunder, Sam was sure it would shake their tiny boat to pieces.

Tony rushed back to the radio, but just as quickly he went back to the controls.

"Give me that," he ordered as he ripped Tyler's hands off the wheel.

"Those things are coming real fast," Sam yelled, as he watched the gathering clouds. "I don't think we're gonna make it back."

"Shut up," Tony barked. "You and Tyler have to grab onto this wheel and keep us going straight west."

"How do we know where west is?" Tyler shrieked.

Tony pointed down. "Watch the compass here. If the needle isn't on the W, turn the wheel 'til it is. If it goes toward the E, start turning it back the other way. If it goes past W toward the S, then crank it back to the right. You got it?"

"I think so," Tyler whimpered.

"I do," Sam said with confidence.

"Good," Tony yelled. "I gotta get back on

the radio."

The wind blew so hard it sprayed water all over Sam and Tyler. Sam noticed the waves were getting more ferocious by the minute. "This isn't good, is it?" he shouted to Tyler.

"I've never been out when it was this rough," he yelled through the roar. "We could really be in trouble."

Even with the howling of the wind, and the waves pounding against the two parts of the boat in the water, Sam could still hear what Tony said.

"Mayday, mayday. This is the catamaran, Shark's Finn, out of Harper's—" He didn't get to say another word because a giant wave crashed into the side of the boat, flooding the cabin. Its power drove the water with such force that it covered everything inside, including the radio, which spit, fizzled, and then died.

"Oh, man!" Tony cried when he scrambled back out on deck. Sam and Tyler did the best they could to hold onto the wheel. Tony strained to pull himself along the rail. When he reached the wheel, he pointed to the compass.

"West! I told you guys *west*. How come we're going east?" he demanded.

"Right now this thing is going wherever the wind wants it to," Sam snapped back at Tony.

No sooner had he said those words when the biggest gust of wind so far hit them from the side. The fury of that blast began tearing the giant sail into lots of smaller strips of cloth. But before it could finish that job, an even bigger gust hit from the opposite side.

The boys heard a crackling sound seconds before the mighty mast broke off like a thin piece of driftwood. As it ripped away from the boat, it took the sail and all of its rope and pulleys into the sea.

Now it was impossible to steer. The waves became much larger, and they looked like they would swallow the boys and their helpless boat alive at any minute. At one time, it felt like they were in a deep canyon, with towering water walls on all sides.

Suddenly there was the feeling of being lifted up in a giant elevator. In only seconds, they found themselves perched on top of a wave so high, if they weren't being pelted with rain, Sam was sure he would be able to see for miles. Then, just as suddenly, their small boat was cast down into the depths again.

After what felt like an hour of riding up and down in the elevator of this ocean skyscraper, all three boys heard another sickening crack. It sounded completely different than when the mast gave way.

Sam never knew he could feel so small, so insignificant, so useless. The angry ocean was more powerful than anything he had ever experienced. For the first time he could remember, Sam was truly terrified.

"Okay, you guys," Tony said, his voice trembling, "we have to choose."

"Choose? Choose what?" Sam scoffed. "I don't see that we have a chance to choose anything except being slapped silly by these waves."

"This thing is gonna break apart."

"Are you sure?" Tyler cried.

Tony nodded. Rain pelted his round face. "Pretty sure."

"So what can we do?" Sam asked.

"We have to decide which part of the boat to get on. When it breaks in two, I don't want any of us to get separated."

"Which one?" Sam asked as he scanned his options.

"It doesn't matter. They're both gonna take a beating in this storm."

"Do you think we'll sink?"

"I hope not. We might as well take the one we're on now. Here, grab a rope and tie it tight around your waist. Tie the other end to the railing. When this baby comes apart, you're on your own." He moved back toward the cabin.

"Where are you going?" Sam demanded.

"I'll pass an extra life jacket out to each of

you, along with rain jackets."

"Rain jackets?" Tyler asked. "We're soaked now."

"Stick the life jacket on your shoulders and pull the rain jacket over it."

"What good is a rain jacket?" Sam demanded. "We got all the rain we need already."

"You can close it up, and then I'll hand you some food to stuff inside. Maybe it won't all end up in the water."

For the next few minutes, Tony passed things to the others. The cracking sound from the boat's body could be heard more often now. Sam looked down just in time to see the boat starting to come apart.

"Hurry, Tony, it's about to let go!"

His friend rushed back out on the deck with something rolled up under one arm. With the other, he pulled himself toward his friends. Another large wave broke across the flat part of the boat, nearly knocking Tony to the deck.

"What's that?" Sam asked.

"It's a rubber life raft, just in case."

"In case of what?"

"Just in case, alright?"

Tony had only finished tying the last knot of his safety rope to the rail when three sets of ears heard a final cracking sound. This one was five times louder than when the mast snapped. The boys watched helplessly as the other side of the boat broke off and blew away from them.

Fortunately, they had chosen the best side to stay on because the other one also had the main deck attached to it. The weight of that deck made the whole thing turn upside down in the water. Then a gust of wind turned it into a giant kite and the whole thing blew away.

But they weren't much better off. Their side bobbed in the water like a soccer ball, first up high on top of the water, then down deep again.

Sam felt too scared to be sick. Right now, he wished he'd told the truth. At least his father would know what to do.

Sam also knew Tony's frantic radio call didn't

tell the Coast Guard anything. All they knew was that some people too stupid to listen to the weather warnings were out in the middle of the ocean, maybe in the middle of a hurricane someplace. But where?

Several times, the waves became so powerful the boys were thrown into the water. Each time, they struggled to pull themselves back onto the safety of what was left of their pitiful little boat.

Sam grew so tired he could hardly make it. The water made his clothes feel so heavy, like one of those deep-sea diving suits with the big metal helmet and boots. "I don't think I can take much more of this," he gasped.

"Just hang on!" Tony shouted.

Sam was glad his friend had thought about the ropes. If he hadn't been fastened to the rail, they would be miles apart from each other by now.

Suddenly the rain stopped. The wind grew calm. The waves continued as big as ever, but it felt like the worst might be over.

"Is that it?" he asked. Then he half laughed and half cried. "We made it, we made it!"

"No, we didn't," Tyler corrected. "We're just in the middle of it. In a few minutes we get to take the same wild ride on the other side of the storm."

"Try and rest up a little," Tony suggested. "You're gonna need it."

Sam thought he'd fallen asleep. For a moment, it felt again like only one of the many bad dreams he'd had the night before. He was sort of right. This was a bad dream, the worst bad dream of his life. *But I might not get to wake up at the end of this one,* he thought.

Then he heard the haunting howl of the wind again. Only a gentle breeze blew where they were right now, but the sound of a hundred freight trains came from just beyond the next mountain of waves. In only minutes, the boys found themselves in the full fury of the raging storm all over again.

A wave bigger than any before flipped the

wreckage they clung to upside down. This made the ropes that had been their safety threaten to keep them under water. Sam pulled at his rope, but it only tightened its grip around the rail beyond his reach. Then, when he thought he'd breathed his last, he said in his mind, *Lord, help us, please!*

As quickly as they had flipped under, the boys suddenly found themselves back upright and facing the full force of the storm once again. The wind blew so hard the water spray felt more like walking into a hail storm. Each drop that hit his face stung the skin. *Right now I'd be happy to be walking anywhere*, he thought.

"Are there any sharks out here?" he called to Tony.

"Oh, I'm sure there are, but those guys are the last thing you should worry about right now. Make sure your ropes are tight."

Sam looked over to check on Tyler just as a brutal wave hit his friend with full force. The power of that blow sent Tyler first into the air, then over the side. "Tony!" Sam screamed.

Tony looked out where Tyler bobbed up and down like a barrel in the water. Sam checked to see that his friend's rope was still tied to the rail. Tony clung to the railing too far away, but Sam was just close enough to reach out and grab Tyler's rope.

He pulled on it as Tyler pulled himself, hand over hand, toward what was left of their boat. When he finally reached the side, he looked too exhausted to climb back on under his own power. So Sam used what little strength he still had to rescue his friend.

"I wish somebody knew where we were," Sam cried.

"Yeah, well they don't," Tony grumbled. "Shoot, I don't even know where we are anymore."

"Where we are is in serious trouble," Sam said.

"Is that supposed to be some kind of a news flash?" Tony shot back.

"You were the one who wanted to keep everything such a deep, dark secret," Sam yelled.

"Well, you didn't have to come, you know."

"Yeah, right. I suppose that would have made a difference."

"You'd be on land right now. Is that different enough?"

Sam felt too worn out to argue any longer. He thought about the soft, warm bed he'd left so early in the morning. He also recalled the lesson he'd learned. *My parents are sure to find out what I did wrong, but I don't think they'll ever find me.*

Then his mind began to play tricks on him. He wondered if they would wash up on some island in the middle of nowhere. *Was there really an Island of Lost Boys, like in Pinocchio?* That notion made him laugh. *Any island we'd find would be an island of at least three lost boys, that's for sure.* When he laughed, he took on a mouthful of water that made him cough.

Then, for no reason at all, he thought of the story of Jonah. That gave him a creepy feeling all over. He searched the waves all around to see if they were about to be swallowed by a great fish.

The big fish made him remember the whale in Pinocchio. On and on his mind raced from one ridiculous thought to the next. The more Sam thought, the weirder things got. So he decided to stop thinking altogether.

After battling for hours, all three boys could fight the storm no longer. One by one they drifted into a sleep deeper than the lowest point the waves had plunged their damaged craft.

Just before everything went completely black, Sam thought, *It couldn't get any worse than this. C . . . could it?*

CHAPTER 11

Alone on Lost Island

Sam had no idea how long the storm lasted or how far they had drifted. The next thing he knew, he still heard what sounded like thunder, only this time the rumble wasn't quite as low and threatening. There was a crashing sound too, but not like in a storm. And it was dark, really dark.

At first, he thought he might have gone blind, or he was dead. Whatever it was, Sam really hoped this was only a dream, but it still wasn't.

The other thing he noticed, when he began moving his tongue around in his mouth, was that it felt like he had eaten his way clear across the sandbox in his neighbor's yard. For the first time, he understood why a clam makes a pearl, to smooth out a jagged piece of sand. From the mouth full of grit, Sam was certain he could make hundreds of pearls.

He was also soaking wet, and every possible part of his body hurt. He wondered if this was what it felt like for a goalie at the end of the National Hockey League championship game.

At first, Sam thought he might be all alone.

Was he the only one to survive the storm? He began to clear the sand from his mouth. There was even a sandy crust around his eyes.

He wished this dream would end soon and he'd find that his water bottle had dumped over again, but he knew better. The more he tried to spit the sand out, the louder the sounds he made.

"Hey, is that you?" Tony groaned.

"Don't try to pull that one on me, 'cause I don't got a mirror on me," Sam sputtered. "Tyler, where's Tyler?"

"I'm over here someplace," a voice half

squeaked and half groaned. "I just don't know where here is yet."

"We'd better get out of the water and try to dry off," Sam suggested. He barely had the strength to pull himself up onto what felt like a sandy beach. He tried again to look around. "Wonder where we are?"

"Lost at sea, that's where," Tony grunted.

"We can't be lost at sea; we're on land."

"So, do you know where we are?"

"No," Sam answered.

"Then we're lost. I'm all wet, so I'm going to guess we're out in the ocean someplace, okay?"

From the tone of Tony's voice, Sam decided not to mess with him.

"I'm cold," Tyler said. Sam heard his teeth chattering.

"Glad to meet you, Cold, I'm Hungry," Tony said.

"Let's just try and get some sleep. Things have got to look brighter in the morning."

"I've always hated it when people said

dumb stuff like that," Tony said. "Every cloud has a silver lining; it's darkest before the dawn. Come on, give me a break."

"Just try to go to … sleep." Sam almost didn't get the word *sleep* out of his mouth before he went completely unconscious.

After what seemed like only an hour, he awoke again. This time, he could hardly open his eyes. His eyelids were completely covered with sand and ocean gunk. He felt it inside his eyes too, and it hurt. As he squinted and then tried to open just one eye, he felt much warmer. It was bright out, the sun was shining, and he heard the gentle sound of waves crashing onto the beach.

Slowly, he worked all the sand out of both eyes. Sand. Sam felt it everywhere.

He strained to rise up on one elbow, then one knee, but he was unable to stand up.

He felt the diving watch still on his wrist. When he held it to his ear, he couldn't hear it ticking. *How stupid. It's a digital.* He opened his eyes again and looked at the face of the watch, but it was covered in sand. When he wiped a little of it off, he saw the numbers one, three, two. "One thirty-two?" he asked. "Can't be."

This time when he tried to stand, he grabbed the rail from the piece of boat that had been the only reason they hadn't drowned. He gave a mighty tug and pulled himself up. He noticed he was still tied to the rail. *Wonder where I'd be if that thing had come loose in the night?*

When he looked around again, he saw Tyler and Tony still sleeping in the sand. A little hermit crab ran right past Tony's nose. "Hey, you guys, we'd better get moving," he warned.

"I'm not going any place," Tony mumbled.

"Me neither," Tyler added. "Somebody might as well dig a hole and bury me right here."

"It's already going on two o'clock in the afternoon. We have to make some plans."

"Plans? I plan to sleep until next week," Tony announced.

"Come on, you guys. Get up. We have to try to fix a shelter or something. I don't think any of us is up for exploring until tomorrow."

"Tomorrow?" Tyler shouted. "What do you mean, tomorrow?"

"Unless you have an idea for getting us out of here," Sam said.

With clumsy hands, he untied his rope and staggered toward a few palm trees and tall grass in the distance. As slow as he moved, it felt like they might as well be a hundred miles away, but he kept pushing himself. About half way there he stopped, turned around, and looked back toward his friends.

Tyler and Tony had also untied their ropes. Tyler was sort of walking, but Tony crawled on the sand like a sea turtle. "Hey, wait up," he called out. No one paid any attention to him.

Sam reached the trees first. It was all he could do to fall into the grass. It felt like a soft mattress under his sore and tired bones. Tyler soon joined him, but Tony had fallen asleep again about half way between them and the water.

"What are we gonna do?" Tyler asked.

"We have to fix a place so we can sleep. That way we can rest up for tomorrow. By morning we should feel a little stronger, I hope."

"I'm really hungry," Tyler complained.

"Me too," Sam answered. "Did any of your food make it?"

Tyler reached into his rain jacket and pulled something out.

"Whatcha got?" Sam asked.

"I think it used to be a bag of crackers, but it's just a sandy, salty mush now. I don't think we can eat it."

"Hey, Tony," Sam called. "You got any food on you?" Tony didn't move and he didn't say a word.

"I'm worried about him," Sam told Tyler. "Think I'll go out and see if I can drag him up here."

"Good luck," Tyler groaned. "Don't forget

how much the guy weighs."

Sam stumbled out to his friend and tried to wake him. "Tony, Tony. You gotta get up and out of this sun. It's a killer, man."

"Go away. Leave me alone," he bellowed. But Sam didn't give up. It took a long time, but he made sure Tony dragged himself up to the shady grass.

Then Sam looked around for a place they could use for shelter. He spotted some large branches on plants that grew near to the ground. "Tyler, can you help me?"

"Help you what?"

"Get some branches to make a place to stay."

"I can try," he groaned. Together, the two boys worked for over an hour to make a shelter in case it rained again. "I'm really getting hungry," Tyler said. "We should look for an old net and try to catch some fish."

"Are you ready to eat them raw? Because if you look around, we don't have a working stove," Tony said.

Sam looked at Tony. "Wait a minute. I'm not eating any raw fish."

"Why not?" Tyler asked.

"You aren't serious?"

"Sure. Just think of it as sushi."

"Sushi? What's sushi?" Sam asked.

"It's raw fish wrapped in leaves and stuff."

Sam shuddered all over. "Are you kidding me?"

"You've never heard of sushi?"

"No, and the closest I'm ever coming to raw fish is a can of tuna."

"See any tuna cans around here?"

"No."

"Well then, raw fish it is."

"We need a fire," Sam said. "A boat might see us at night if we have one."

"A boat never saw anybody," Tony sneered, "and besides, I'm fresh out of matches."

"I remember seeing a video about starting a fire with sticks," Tyler said.

"You mean by rubbing them together real

fast?" Sam asked.

"Yeah."

"Do you think we can make that work?"

"We could take turns. At least we can try," Tyler suggested.

The boys found several dry sticks under a dead tree. Sam gathered dry grass and a few scraps of wood splinters. For what seemed like hours they tried and tried to get the sticks hot enough to start a fire by spinning one of them as fast as it would go into a hole in the side of the other one. Then, finally, Sam yelled, "That's it. I quit!"

"It might be just about to work," Tyler pleaded.

"No, it isn't going to work. I said I give up."

"Here, let me take another turn," Tyler said. As he scrambled over to grab the sticks out of Sam's hand, Tony asked, "Hey, what's that?"

"What's what?" Sam asked, looking down at the sticks.

"There, on the ground."

Tyler looked in the sand. He reached down and picked up something shiny. "It's my stamp magnifying glass. I can't believe it made it through that storm."

"Now we're getting somewhere," Sam said with a new surge of hope.

"I'm right where I've been all afternoon," Tony grumbled.

"Tyler," Sam said, "Get some more dry grass and sticks, and hand me your magnifier."

"What for?"

"Just do it," Sam pleaded. He moved into an area where the sun shined so bright, it made the sand feel hot enough to cook dinner on, if they had any dinner to cook on it, which they didn't. Tyler came back with bits and pieces of all the dry material he could hold. "Stick it in one big pile," Sam directed.

"I still don't get what you're trying to do," Tyler complained.

"Just watch me."

By this time, Tony had become curious and

dragged himself toward the others. Sam held the magnifying glass close to the dead leaves, twigs, and grasses Tyler had found. He placed it close enough until there was a very bright pinpoint of light shining on one of the biggest dead leaves. That point of light was so bright it hurt to look at it, so Tyler and Tony turned away.

"I smell smoke," Tony hollered. "Isn't that smoke I smell?" When he and Tyler looked again, Sam was already blowing on the stack of leaves while he pushed more grass under the bright light. Then, suddenly, the pile burst into flames. "It's . . . a . . . miracle!" Tony shouted.

"No, it's science. But, if you want to think I can do miracles, that's okay with me," Sam said with a laugh. "Now we have to get more wood, enough to last us through the night."

"I wish we had some food," Tyler cried.

"Did somebody say food?" Tony asked in a sly voice.

Both Sam and Tyler stopped what they were

doing and looked straight at him. Tony reached into this rain jacket pocket and pulled out a plastic bag of crackers and a can of sardines.

"Oh, man," Sam complained. "Did it have to be sardines? I hate those smelly fish." He waved his arms around in the air. "There must be a gazillion fish in the ocean, but no, you gotta bring a can of those wretched things with you."

"Nobody said you had to eat them, but we don't have anything else on the menu," Tony told them. "And the crackers are mostly dust now. But at least it's something." The sardine can had a self-opening top. That was good since no one brought a can opener along. Tony opened it, releasing that awful smell Sam hated so much.

Tony passed the can around after chugging down four fish in a row. Tyler was next. While he took his sardines out of the can, Tony dumped some of the cracker crumbs into his hand and ate them.

Now it was Sam's turn. He clamped his nose closed in order to try and block the smell and the taste. It almost worked, but he could still taste them, and it nearly made him gag.

Then he and Tyler finished the cracker dust. Tony took the last remaining crumbs, dumped them into the sardine juice, and ate it like a mud pie.

The taste was rough on Sam, but at least he wouldn't starve. "Wish I had a big iced tea right now," he said.

"With lemon and sugar?" Tyler added.

"Yeah, those fish and crackers were really salty."

"Water, water everywhere . . ." Tony said, looking out toward the ocean.

"Ain't that the truth," Sam sighed. "Hurry up," he reminded them. "We'd better get that wood. It's gonna be dark soon."

This time all three boys felt strong enough to help. Before long, they had a big stack of dead branches and a few pieces of larger driftwood.

Sam looked at the pile. "That should do it."

He built a roaring fire. Then each boy did his best to make a bed out of the grassy area under their shelter.

Sam had been right. It was quickly getting dark again. "I'll stay awake as long as I can and watch the fire," he said. "Then I'll wake one of you guys up to keep an eye on it."

Tony and Tyler settled into their new beds. "It could be a lot worse," Tony suggested.

"Yeah," Sam added. "Our dads could be here right now. That would be a lot worse."

"Boy oh boy," Tyler sighed, "I'm gonna be so grounded."

"Me too," Sam said. "I'll be grounded 'til I'm dead, and wait 'til your dad finds out about his busted boat, Tony."

"Remind me to remember to forget you said that," Tony groaned.

CHAPTER 12

Survival

Having the first fire watch gave Sam a lot of time to think. But by morning he was so wiped out he couldn't remember if he had changed with anyone else for fire watch or not.

He heard the gentle pounding of waves on the beach not far from where he'd been sleeping. The air was warm, and based on how hard it was to see right away, he figured the sun was already far up in the sky.

Most importantly, he could still smell smoke. That meant at least the fire hadn't gone out in the night.

As soon as his eyes adjusted and he was able to look around, he noticed his friends weren't anywhere nearby. *Did I dream they made it when they didn't? Are . . . they . . .*

"Hey, you old sea slug," Tony bellowed as he flopped down in the grass. "I'm pretty sure this is Lost Island."

Sam sat all the way up. "It's lost all right. I think now, with us on it, it might as well be The Island of Lost Boys. Three of them anyway."

"Well, we are lost," Tony said.

"We're not lost. God knows where we are, even if nobody else does."

Just then Tyler walked up. "What should we do?" he asked.

Now Sam remembered he had decided in the night that it was up to him to take charge. They couldn't count on Tony to be much help and Tyler did everything Tony said or did, so that made him undependable too.

Sam stood up and brushed the sand from his legs. "I think, first, we need to explore close by our campsite. We should split up to see what we can find. Tyler, why don't you go that way?" Sam pointed down the beach in one direction. "And, Tony, you go that way. I'll walk around in the trees and bushes and try to find something to eat."

"Oh, yeah, do that. I've never been this hungry before, ever," Tony complained as he held his stomach.

"Since I'm the only one with a watch, and it still works, I'll come back onto the beach in about an hour. I'll signal for you to come back and report what you've seen."

"What if we find something earlier?" Tyler asked.

"If you can carry it, bring it back right away. If you can't, come get us. We need something to store fresh water in, something to cook with if you find it, and a net for catching fish. Okay, let's split up."

The young explorers began walking in opposite directions, hoping to find something, anything to take away their hunger pains or help get them off this island.

It seemed a little crazy, but Sam pretended

to be the first person ever to discover the island.

One of the first things he found was a little place where a few large rocks seemed piled together. At the top of one he found a shape almost like the large mixing bowl his mother used to mix a triple batch of chunky peanut butter cookies. Right now he really didn't need that thought in his head. Worse yet, he could almost smell them baking in the oven back home. That made his mouth water.

"Man, I wish I'd done the right thing," he said out loud. "Then I'd still be safe at home." When he looked into the bowl shaped rock, he noticed it was full of water. *That had to come from the rain.* He dipped in one finger, pulled it out, and tasted. "Ummm . . . not salty." Then he scooped out more and drank it. "Ah. . . ."

In the same area, he found several more places where water had collected among the rocks. *At least we won't die of thirst,* he decided.

Next, he saw something strange. He thought they looked a little like bananas, but they hung upside down in the trees. Sam had only seen bananas in small clumps at the grocery store, or when his mother brought them home. But, from where he was standing, he could see hundreds of them.

On the ground nearby were several brown and green shapes that looked like rocks or bowling balls. Sam remembered his dad talking about the coconuts he'd eaten on one of his research projects. *That's what these are.*

He gathered a few bunches of green bananas and two of the coconuts. When he looked at his watch, he'd only been gone about twenty minutes, but since his search had been so successful, he decided to head back to camp.

Just as he plunked his treasures on the ground, he thought he heard Tyler's voice far off in the distance. When he looked down the beach, he could just barely see his friend. Tyler looked as small as an ant, but he was waving his hands wildly in the air, and screaming like a fog horn. Sam took off running toward him.

Tony followed farther back.

As he got closer Sam heard Tyler yell, "You gotta come see this. You aren't going to believe it."

"Believe what?" Sam shouted.

Tyler kept jumping up and down in the sand. "A boat! I found a boat!"

Tony ran up in time to hear the word, boat. "Boat? Did you say something about a boat?"

"Yes, I found one."

"We're saved!" Tony shouted.

"Well," Tyler said, "not exactly."

"What do you mean?" Sam asked.

"It's only part of a boat, and it's sticking out of the water."

Sam rushed off as he called out over his shoulder, "Come on, show us."

The boys sprinted a little farther down the beach until they reached a small cove shaped like a half moon and saw the boat. All three boys came to a stop at the same time and just stared out at the wreck.

"Who's gonna go out and see what's in there?" Tyler asked.

"Tony, you should do it," Sam suggested. "You're the one who knows the most about boats."

"Me? I'm not going near that thing. Man, there could be dead people inside."

"Really?" Tyler shrieked as he stepped back and fell over a large piece of driftwood.

"Sure, it probably got caught in the same storm that brought us here," Tony said.

"Well, I'm not afraid," Sam said in defiance. He waded out into the water. Soon he swam toward a boat that looked as if it had turned completely upside down. The rudder that steered it stuck up in the air too. He knew for sure he wasn't swimming toward a sailboat because this one was flatter on the bottom.

Sam made his way around the other side, then yelled, "There's a great big hole on this side." He peered inside, but there wasn't any way to get into the cabin from there. So he swam around to the back. Now he was glad he'd taken the scuba class because they had spent so much time doing breathing exercises. The experience from swimming underwater in the final test would be very helpful to him now.

Sam looked into the water and thought he saw a door. He took long, deep breaths as he prepared to dive. Then under the water he went. The salt hurt his eyes a little, but he was able to see that the door into the cabin, even though it was under water, was open. When he couldn't hold his breath any longer he swam for the surface.

"I'm goin' in," he called out to the others. Again, he took deep breaths, then disappeared beneath the waves once more. This time he used the sides of the door opening to pull himself into the cabin. His head popped up inside where a large pocket of air allowed him to breathe normally. Immediately, he gulped in precious air.

He wasn't up by the ceiling because, since

the boat had tipped over, that part was now the floor and the floor was the ceiling.

Then he heard something odd. He could faintly hear Tyler screaming in a muffled tone, "He's dead, I know it. Sam drowned in that death trap."

From the sound of Tyler's voice, Sam knew he really meant what he said, but it made him laugh anyway. He decided to stay a little longer.

As he looked around, it was a relief that there weren't any dead people inside. And it looked like most of what used to be in the cabin must have been flushed out in the storm, or when it flipped over.

He felt around with his feet, which stood around a light fixture on the . . . ceiling. One of his feet kicked something, and whatever it was broke apart. Now his feet felt several objects he thought might be cans.

He reached down and grasped one, but when he pulled it out of the water, the label had already soaked off. *Wonder what's inside*, he thought. *Better not be more sardines.*

He imagined it might be beef stew, chicken noodle soup, or spaghetti. Then another thought quickly followed. He held up the can, shook it, and said out loud, "I sure hope they didn't have a dog." The sound of his voice made it seem like he was talking with his head in a big bucket, and that made him smile.

When he turned around, he spotted something that would change their stay on the island one hundred percent. Hanging upside down, next to the door was a bright red fire ax. Sam thought of all kinds of ways they could use it. He grabbed the ax in one hand, held one of the metal cans in the other, and dove under the water to swim out the door again.

As his head broke through the surface of the water outside the boat, Sam was pretty sure he could hear Tyler crying. That made him feel bad. He remembered reading about Tom Sawyer and how the whole town thought he was dead. They even had a funeral for him.

Sam decided he wouldn't go off and hide to make his friends think he was dead. That would be mean, plus he was way too excited to show them the treasures he'd discovered.

"Hey, guys!" he yelled as he thrashed in the water while holding up the ax. Tyler looked up. His sad face changed the instant he saw his friend. "Look what I found," Sam hollered. His voice echoed in the small cove.

"Sam, you made it; you're not dead," Tyler called back.

"I don't think I am," Sam said with a laugh. As his feet found bottom, he walked out of the water. In one hand, he raised the ax and in the other, the mysterious can.

"What's in the can?" Tony asked. "And don't play with me."

"Not sardines, I hope," Sam repeated.

"Let's take it up on the beach and bust it open with that ax," Tyler pleaded.

They went to the weathered piece of driftwood Tyler had fallen over. The log had a spot where another branch used to be. It was a perfect spot to hold the can.

Tony smacked his lips. "I'm voting for beef stew."

"I hope they didn't have a dog," Tyler suggested. "It could be dog food."

"I thought the same thing out there. We just gotta think positive," Sam said.

Tyler's face wrinkled as he covered his mouth with one hand. Then he mumbled, "Well, I'm *positive* I'm not eatin' any dog food, that's for sure."

Sam placed the can in the special slot in the wood. Then he carefully raised the ax slightly above it. With one smooth, downward motion, the ax cut a slot clear across the lid. Out sprayed brown juice and several brown beans.

"Beans! You brought us a can of beans?" Tony complained.

"Hey, at least it's not dog food."

"What else did you find?" Tyler asked.

"Just a whole bunch more of these cans."

"Great," Tony groaned. "Beans for breakfast, beans for lunch, beans for dinner . . . somebody help this bunch." That made everyone laugh.

Sam and the others took several trips out to the wreck to see what else they could find. Unfortunately, only the cans of beans had survived the storm. After they brought all the cans to shore, Tyler found a torn fishing net in the sand. He piled the cans onto it. Then each boy grabbed a side and they carried the load back to camp.

"Did you find anything on your part of the beach?" Sam asked Tony.

"Nothing but sand."

"I forgot to tell you guys, but I found water, bananas, and coconuts, I think."

"You did? Where? I am so hungry and thirsty." Just then, the idea of beans didn't sound so bad after all. Sam thought it would be good to have a hot meal, and they could use the cans for saving more fresh water.

The day passed quickly. The boys gathered

and cut more wood with their new ax. Sam used it to open several coconuts. After drinking the sweet liquid from inside, he used one of the can lids to scoop out the delicious, sweet, white coconut meat.

The bananas were still too green, so Sam hung a few bunches on the side of their shelter.

"With this ax, we can make a better shelter," he announced. From then until nearly dark, Sam cut several pieces of small dead branches and logs into equal sizes. "Tomorrow we'll make a hut."

"Do you know how to build a hut?" Tony asked.

"No, but how hard could it be?"

As darkness settled over the island, it looked like the sun went down on the horizon right into the water. "How does the sun do that?" Sam asked.

"Do what?"

"Look like it goes under the water?"

"It doesn't," Tony said. "The thing just goes

to the other side of the earth. Don't worry; it'll be back in the morning."

Sam watched the sun as it continued to sink slowly into the water like a giant, orange beach ball.

"I'm gonna miss it," Tyler sighed.

Sam built the fire bigger than the night before because now, with his new ax, he had all the firewood he needed. The warm glow from the fire made everyone feel safer. Out in the distance, far from the island, lightning could be seen flashing up in the sky.

"Think it'll rain on us again?" Tyler asked.

"That stuff is going in the opposite direction," Tony answered.

"Tomorrow we need to finish our shelter. Then we have to make a fire holder," Sam instructed.

"What's a fire holder?" Tony asked.

"Something to carry a few coals in if we have to move our camp or if the rain drowns out our main fire. In the morning, I'll look for something to put it in."

"You think it'll take the whole day to do that?" Tyler asked.

"No. After we do the shelter and the coals we need to see what's on the other side of this island. If we can find a high enough place, we might be able to make a signal from there. He looked out toward the water. "I wonder if anyone is looking for us."

"They wouldn't know where to start," Tony said. "I didn't get to finish my radio distress call, and none of our families know where we went."

Still, the boys were beginning to feel better about their chances. They had food; there was plenty of fresh rainwater, a warm fire, and more than enough beans.

"Do you think there's anyone else on this island?" Tyler asked.

"I sure hope n . . . um, I mean, I don't think so," Sam stammered. Right now, more than anything else, he wished he'd told his parents the truth. *How can they ever forgive me?* he wondered.

CHAPTER 13

Shark Boats & Scary Men

Each of the boys took a turn at fire watch. When Sam's second turn came, it couldn't have been any darker. He threw a few more pieces of wood on the fire so light from the dancing flames flickered in a wider circle. He heard the waves crashing onto the beach in the distance and shuddered. *I wonder what it must be like to drift around out there in the dark.* That thought made him scoot closer to the fire. It made his face hot, but somehow he felt a little safer.

Looking up into the black sky, the stars looked brighter than any time he'd looked at them before. A chill came over him, but it wasn't from the night air. Even at night, the weather was comfortably warm.

Sam wondered if he and his friends would ever escape. Would they have to spend the rest of their lives alone on this place? He felt so alone with all that water lapping up on every inch of the island sand. He'd heard about how some of the people who live in a place like Hawaii feel closed in and isolated from the rest of the world. Right now that was exactly how he felt.

By morning, they all were well rested. Sam checked the bananas and found a few that had turned a little yellow and were just starting to ripen. He decided to save the beans for later.

Soon the new shelter began to take shape. Sam chose a spot where he could use two trees for the first posts, and then constructed posts for two more corners. He added another post in the center. He and his friends built a house on stilts by tying other branches together with vines.

They set the floor in place using stronger sticks and tied those to the cross pieces of wood with more vines, and strips of bark Sam had cut with the ax. He'd seen a man do the same thing on a survival show on TV.

Then they used the same materials to make a frame for their roof. On top of that, they placed several palm branches and tied those down to the frame.

Next, Sam designed a three-sided shelter on the ground to protect their valuable fire. He took one of the bean cans and punched a hole in each side near the top with the sharp point of his ax. Then he slipped a stick through the holes to make a handle. He scooped up some sand and poured it into the bottom of the can. On top of that he placed a few dry leaves and small sticks.

No one had paid any attention to the time, but they thought it must be past noon because they were hungry again. Sam had been so busy he hadn't looked at the watch until now. "Lunch break," he called out.

"Not more beans," Tony grunted.

"Got any better ideas?"

"Yeah, a lot of them, except none of 'em are on this island at the moment."

"Then hot beans it is," Sam told them. Earlier, he'd found a couple of sticks that came to a Y at the top. He pushed those into the soft sand and placed a longer stick on top of them that stretched across the fire. With a piece of wire they found on the boat, Sam fastened that to holes he'd made in the bean can. He slipped the wire over the long stick, and lowered the can of beans over the warm fire. In no time, the brown beans bubbled. That's when he knew they were ready.

After lunch, they decided to begin their hike across to the other side. Only Sam had gone exploring into the island before. The others had spent their time searching the beach areas. The island had sharp rocks running out to the water in both directions from their campsite, making it impossible to walk around them.

The boys found walking sticks and were soon on their way. "There sure are a lot of different plants in here," Tyler said as he looked all around. "How do plants and trees get on an island?"

"I don't know about all of them, but I read that some of the plants get started with the birds' help," Sam said.

"Birds? What do they have to do with it?" Tony said.

"Well, what do most birds eat?" Sam asked.

"Worms and bugs?" Tyler asked.

"And?" Sam asked.

"A bunch of stuff with seeds in them," Tony answered.

"That's right. Then the birds fly around, and . . . you know."

Tyler stopped walking. "You're kidding!" he gasped.

"No, I'm not. Then some of the seeds come from boats, packages, the wind, and big storms like the one that brought us here. There are all kinds of ways plants can get started."

"Did you see any animals when you went

back here?" Tony wanted to know.

"Not actually seen them, but I've heard some noises. Mostly up in the trees. And there are lots of birds."

The boys came to a place that looked like some of the jungle movies Sam had seen.

"Are we going to see some guy swinging from those vines up there?" Tony mocked.

"You can be sure of it," Sam said with a wink. And before Tyler could let out one of his famous whining cries, Sam sprinted over to the nearest vine, grabbed it with both hands while still running full speed, and swung out over a low spot in the ground. The force of his weight carried him about twenty feet, then he came back and dropped to the sand.

"I meant anyone besides us," Tony complained.

"Come on, guys." Sam motioned with one arm and said, "The big rocks are over this way." He led the way deeper into the jungle. Soon the boys climbed jagged rocks, going almost straight up at times.

"We should have brought some water," Tony said, huffing and puffing.

Sam tried to encourage his friends. "I think it's just a little farther, then we can rest at the top."

It took them another ten or fifteen minutes, but they finally came out of the thick jungle onto what looked like the highest point on the entire island.

"Man," Tony nagged. "A guy can see for miles from up here, and what can he see? Nothing for miles and miles from up here."

Sam shrugged, "What'd you expect? It's an island."

As they scanned the beach for any signs of life beside themselves, Tyler noticed something. "Hey, look down there." He pointed toward another cove, much larger than the one where the damaged boat had washed up. This cove was large enough that the water stayed calmer there too.

"We should come over here and go swimming and fishing," he said. "At least we wouldn't get beat to death with waves like at our camp."

Sam crossed his arms over his chest, and took a deep breath. "It would take us a full day just to carry stuff one way."

"So what," Tony interrupted, "It looks like a better campsite than we have now, and if help does come, a boat would have a better chance of getting in there, and back out."

Suddenly Sam shouted, "Look!" He pointed way out in the ocean.

"What?" the others asked together as they strained to see what Sam saw.

"Can't you see it? Way out there. I think I see a boat, and it's heading this way . . . fast!"

As hard as they tried, neither Tony nor Tyler could see anything except the waves and the nearly blinding reflection of the sun on the water.

Then Sam added, "I can hear them too."

"I see two of them, and they're heading straight for that cove down there."

"I think you've been in the sun a little too long," Tony teased.

Just then Tyler exclaimed, "I hear it too! We're saved! We're saved!" He jumped, screamed, and waved his arms around like a wild man.

"Over here! Over here!" Tony called.

"There are two of them," Tyler said. He watched a little longer and added, "Those are really fast boats."

"Did you say . . . boats?" Tony asked.

"He's right," Sam said. "I see two of them, and they're heading straight for that cove down there."

"Let's run down to the beach so they can see us better," Tony yelled as he began running toward the other side of the rocks they had climbed.

The others joined in, climbing down to where Sam hoped they could get help. Once they'd climbed down from the rocks, the going became much more difficult, with jungle more dense than the way they had gone up.

"I can still hear them," Sam called out. "They're loud, and boy am I glad they are."

The three lost sailors were about to break out of the heavy jungle and burst onto the beach when Sam saw something through the branches of the last few trees. Without warning, he dove into the air and crumpled Tony and Tyler to the ground like he was the most valuable linebacker in all the NFL.

Tony came up first, spitting sand from his mouth, and he was ready for a fight. "What in the world do you think you're doing?" he yelled.

"Yeah," Tyler added with a slight whimper, "Tony fell on me. He could have broken my neck or something."

"I'm sorry, guys, but I had to."

"Well, just wait 'til you see what I have to do," Tony threatened with a clinched fist.

"No, honest. Take a closer look at those boats. Something's not right."

The boys crawled on their hands and knees

like Navy Seals, low to the ground 'til they came to a fallen log. From there, they had a better view, without the people in the boats being able to see them. What they saw frightened all of them.

The boats were painted jet black. Each one had the face of a shark painted on the front with blood on the teeth. The boats carried at least five men each. They were also dressed completely in black.

A chill swept through Sam. As his eyes focused on those teeth covered in blood, he remembered the phone call back at the welcome center.

"What do you think?" Tyler whispered to the others.

"I think I wish I hadn't seen this," Tony whispered back.

The boats slowed as they entered the mouth of the cove. The low rumble of their powerful, jet-like engines made a sickening echo across the water. White smoke billowed from shiny, chrome exhaust pipes that pointed straight up toward the sky.

The boys could hear the men talking and laughing now, only there was too much noise from the engines to be able to hear what they said.

All they could do was watch as one of the men walked out onto the front of the first boat, held his arm up like he was going to change the channels on a big screen TV. While he lowered his arm, two huge bushes at the edge of the beach, where the boats were heading, began to open like the gate of a millionaire's estate. Behind it, Sam could make out the beginning of a channel dug into the side of a hill.

"We need to go down for a better look," Sam said.

"You mean *you* need to," Tony said. "I need to stay right here."

"Yeah," Tyler added. "My mom would want me to hide behind this log; I know she would."

"That's up to you guys," Sam sighed.

"What's the name of that tuna character they call chicken of the sea? It reminds me of you two."

"That does it," Tony grumbled. "Nobody calls me a chicken and gets away with it."

"Whatever it takes to make you come along with me, I don't care. We can settle things later. Now come on, both of you."

"I know I'm not gonna like this," Tyler whined.

After the boats had cleared the back of the bushes, they began to close behind them. Now the boys were able to run along the beach without being seen.

When they came to the place where the movable bushes blocked the channel, they found it was impossible to go around, over, or through them.

"Now what?" Tony asked.

"We go under," Sam said.

"Under? Are you crazy?" Tyler asked.

"Those guys are up to something," Sam

said. "We gotta find out what it is." He broke off long pieces from some of the plants that grew in the water. "I saw this once on TV," he told them.

"The wimpy garden shows you watch are none of our business," Tony muttered.

"It wasn't a garden show. It was about sneaking up on animals in the wild. These are reeds. They're hollow in the center, like a straw."

"Now I get it," Tony said with a wide grin.

"I don't," Tyler grumbled.

Tony turned to Sam. "Like sissy snorkeling."

Sam didn't respond. "Here," he instructed. "You put the fat part in your mouth and put your head under. As long as you keep the other end sticking out of the water, everything will be fine."

"You mean Tony's right?" Tyler asked.

"Yeah, except there's no ball at the top to keep water out if your reed goes under. And it's not for sissies. This is the only way we can sneak up on those guys in there."

"Gotcha."

"So we go in, and then what?" Tony asked.

"That's where you come in. You hang around your dad's marina all the time, right?

"Well, yeah."

"Haven't you seen his mechanics work on the engines at least a thousand times?"

"Oh, now I get it. You want me to wreck their motors, right?"

A knowing smile came to Sam's face as he nodded his approval. "Exactly right. Especially if they're doing what I think they're doing."

The boys put the reeds in their mouths, slipped silently under the water like three alligators and began their dangerous swim. Each kept his reed sticking out of the water. When they came to the bush doors, it was simple to slip under to the other side.

Sam popped his head out of the water and took a quick look around. The boats were parked not very far away. The men were not near them, but the boys could hear their voices.

As the boys dropped under the water again and swam closer, Sam's heart pounded harder and harder. He wondered if the sound hurt his friend's ears, or if the fish heard it. When they reached the back of the first boat, all three boys quietly came to the surface.

They heard one of the men in the distance say with an evil laugh, "After we get this stuff to the mainland, it'll be worth a fortune."

"I don't see anyone," Tony whispered.

"Good," Sam answered. "Hurry up there and do your magic."

Tony climbed up the first small ladder. He crouched down beside the engine compartment and flipped the latch. The whole thing raised up on its own to reveal two car-sized engines, side-by-side.

"Wow!" Tony whispered. Then he pulled wires from both engines, and threw them into the water. They sank to the bottom right away. Tony softly closed the first compartment and made his way across to the second boat where he did exactly the same thing.

Then, without warning, Tyler called out in a hoarse voice just above a whisper, "Someone's coming!"

Tony tossed the second handful of wires into the water, closed the compartment, and scampered to the ladder at the back of that boat. As he climbed down, Sam handed him his reed. "Good job," he whispered.

Tony again entered the water next to his friends. They could hear several people talking, heading back toward the boats. Then, just before the three boys disappeared beneath the surface of the water, Sam saw one of the men. "The guy from the welcome center," he whispered.

"What?" Tony asked.

Sam shook his head. "Never mind. It's a long story." Then he pointed down to the water. The boys disappeared again and swam slowly toward the exit, trying not to make any waves.

Tony made it under the bush barrier okay. But when Tyler tried to go under, his reed did too.

Tyler burst out of the water, gasping and choking for air. That's when Sam surfaced too, just in time to see all those men looking straight at them. He grabbed his friend by the arm and commanded, "Come on, Tyler."

Tony had already cleared the gate and waited on the other side of the bushes in the safety of the calm cove waters.

Sam looked back toward the men and gasped, "They spotted us! We gotta get out of here!"

CHAPTER 14

The Terrifying Chase

Sam had a feeling that they had stumbled onto something big, even compared to the adventures Tony was known for. They struggled to get out of the water as the two secret bushes began to open.

Out of their jaws, like a swarm of mosquitoes, came an army of one-man rubber boats with powerful outboard motors. And they were headed straight toward Sam and the others.

"Hurry you guys; they're right on top of us!" Sam cried out. The boys scrambled onto the beach and quickly made their way to the first line of small bushes and plants in the jungle. As he looked back, Sam saw that the little boats traveled so fast they had already come to rest far up on the beach. The men, still dressed in black, leaped from their boats and ran toward the boys.

"I don't think they can run as fast as we can," Sam said. "Plus, I'll bet they've never come through this way before, and we have."

"How do you know?" Tyler asked.

"I don't, but think about it, why would they?"

"Yeah, but they're gonna catch us for sure," Tyler cried.

"Not if we hurry. We should be able to outrun them."

"But I'm too slow," Tony said.

Sam couldn't remember ever running this hard or this fast before. The muscles in his legs already burned, and it was harder to breathe. But his friends kept close behind him, even Tony.

Soon they reached the thick part of the jungle. Here the going got even slower, but they continued to run as hard as they could.

Then Sam held up his hand. "Stop," he whispered. Together they listened, but didn't hear anyone coming. Sam motioned to his friends and they began the steep, difficult climb to the top of the rocky hill that separated their safe side of the island from the dangerous side. They didn't stop clawing their way until reaching the top where they crouched down behind some branches.

All three were now breathing like they'd just finished a triathlon. "Can . . . you . . . see . . . anything?" Tony asked as he tried to get enough oxygen.

"I can see a bunch of guys dressed in black who look really mad."

"I don't like the sound of that," Tyler groaned.

"Well, at least they're down there and we aren't."

"Sure, but what's to keep them from coming over this big hill to get us?" Tony asked. "Or worse, they could sneak around the island at night, with their big boats and get us in our sleep."

Tyler sat straight up. "They can do that?"

Sam turned to Tony. "Don't you remember? You fixed it so those black boats won't be going anywhere."

"Oh, yeah," Tony chuckled. "I almost forgot about that. I was so scared."

"Now what do we do?" Tyler asked. "They could still use the little boats to come get us."

"He's right," Tony said. "I mean, those guys *know* we're here, and they know we saw them."

"They'll probably know we wrecked their boats too," Tyler added.

"We have to get back and pull our campsite away from the beach. We can't leave anything that would let them know what part of the island we're on."

"What about the fire?"

"We'll have to move it, and our camp, as far into the jungle as we can."

"I really don't like the sound of that," Tyler

cried. "There's creepy, crawly, furry things in the jungle."

"Unless you want to spend the night with those goons down there," Sam said.

Tyler gulped. "No, thank you!"

"Then let's get to it."

It was difficult again, trudging down through the rocks and underbrush, but at least they were walking down and not up. That made the going a little easier. After fighting their way through the final stretch of jungle plants, the boys arrived back into the open, not far from their camp.

"Wait!" Sam whispered. He motioned for everyone to get down.

"What is it?" Tony asked. Tyler just stood there and quivered.

"I think I saw something," Sam said.

Tyler grabbed Sam's arm and held on tight. "Saw what? Where?"

"Something dark, and it was moving around inside our hut."

"Oh, man," Tyler whined. "It's one of them." He released Sam's arm, sank down, and sat in the sand. He put his head in his hands and asked, "Why did we come out here without permission? Why didn't we at least tell somebody?"

"It's too late for that now. I think those guys beat us back here," Tony said.

"How do you figure?" Sam asked.

"Well, while we were coming through the middle of the island, they must have hurried around with those little speedboats and found our stuff." When Tony said that, he and Tyler had their backs to the campsite, and faced Sam.

Sam looked beyond his friends, over at their shelter and began to laugh.

"There's nothin' funny about dying on an island," Tony said in protest. But that didn't matter, Sam just doubled over and laughed even harder. Slowly, the other two boys turned their heads to see what was so funny. When they did, they couldn't believe what they saw. Six, maybe seven monkeys were having a picnic out of the ripe bananas that had been hanging in the tree.

"Where did they come from?" Tyler asked as he stood up again.

"They were probably watching us for the first couple days. Monkeys can be pretty smart," Sam said. "Probably just waited, let us do all the work, then they decided to have a party in our shelter. Come on, we still have to tear the place down."

When the boys came to the entrance of their shelter, the monkeys took one look at them, quickly glanced at each other, looked back at the boys, then screamed like *they* were watching a scary movie. But as the monkeys scrambled to get out of the shelter, the boys also screamed and ran away. When they came to a stop, all three of them started laughing. But the monkeys continued running away into the jungle.

"I'd like to take one of those furry guys home

with me," Tyler sighed.

"Oh, yeah, great idea," Tony said. "Then you could have something to blame whenever you make a mess."

"One of my neighbors had a monkey where I used to live," Sam said. "Monkeys are bad news in a house. They tear up everything in sight, plus they smell really awful. Come on, let's get started."

They walked back toward the shelter and began to pull it apart. Each section had to be dragged back into the bushes, out of sight, and covered with brush and branches. At least it was quicker to destroy it than it was to build it.

Sam took his bean can and prepared to move the fire. After he had placed the best hot coals he could find into the can, he covered the rest of the fire on the ground with sand. *Good thing it doesn't get cold here at night.*

"Shhh," Tony said, warning them. "I think I hear something." They hid deeper in the jungle, but Sam was pretty sure what they heard was the sound of a power boat coming around to their side of the island.

"I thought you knew how to break their boats," Sam said.

Tony raised his hands and shrugged. "I don't understand it. They must have had some spare parts hidden out here."

The boys continued hiding until the sound faded into the distance.

When the boys thought they were safe again, Tyler said, "Whew! That could have been a close one."

"Well, let's set up our new camp. It won't be light much longer," Sam ordered.

This time, all they could do was make soft places to sleep on the ground out of branches and banana leaves. There wasn't time to rebuild the shelter, and they didn't dare make a fire. Sam had decided to keep the coals going in his bean can by adding small pieces of wood as the older embers burned down. At least they could still build a fire if they needed to.

To say the boys slept over the next several hours wouldn't be exactly true. The jungle sounds kept all of them awake. They wondered if the monkeys would come back, or the men dressed in those black suits. And it was still important for someone to keep the portable fire going all night.

"Do you think our parents are looking for us?" Tony asked.

"Yeah, so they can punish us for being so stupid," Tyler answered.

"Well, whatever they're doing, I know they all miss us."

"Speak for yourself," Tyler grumbled.

"What do you mean?"

Tyler's voice softened. "Never mind."

"I've been thinking," Sam began.

Tony sighed. "About what?"

"About a plan."

"I like the sound of this," Tyler added. "What is it?"

"Those guys back there are hiding

something."

"Oh, really?" Tony asked sarcastically.

"Okay, bad choice of words, but now we know it."

"What do we know?" Tyler asked.

"I'm not sure exactly, but not only did we see their secret place, they know we saw it. They've spent a lot of time and money trying to hide whatever it is they're up to."

"So?" Tony asked.

"So, they aren't just going to let us swim away and expect we won't tell anybody what we saw."

"What *did* we see?" Tyler asked. "I'm still not sure what it was."

"They don't know what we saw either," Sam said, "but I think they'll try to keep everything covered up. I know they wouldn't want anyone to find out about the secret entrance."

In a shaky voice, Tony began, "Then you're saying you think they'll come looking until they find us?"

"For sure!"

"So what do we do?"

"We've kept our coals going in the bean can. Right now we should get as much sleep as we can because, in the morning, we need to go back down to our beach and pick up all the junk we can find."

"What kind of junk?" Tyler asked.

"Anything made out of plastic or rubber. Look for tarps, plastic bottles, old tires; things like that."

"Then what?"

"We set up a bunch of fires on the beach."

"Well then, why don't we make it easier on those guys?" Tony said. "We should just go out there and lie on the sand. We could start screaming and yelling, 'Here we are, come get us!'" Tony grumbled.

"No," Tyler interrupted, "I think I get it. They won't know where to look for us. All those fires will confuse them."

"Right, but at the same time, if anyone *is*

still looking for us, the black smoke should help them find where we are."

It wasn't easy, but all three boys managed to get a little sleep. For Sam, it wasn't exactly restful, and he wondered if it had been the same for his friends. It took longer for bright sunlight to pierce through the thick jungle after it hit the beach, so the boys waited until they could see the path before they felt it was safe to walk on it.

Back on the beach, they moved quickly. Sam barked out orders like an army drill sergeant. "Tony, Tyler, go down both sides of the beach. Grab anything you can find that might make black smoke."

While they were gone, Sam ran back and forth between the beach and the jungle. Each time he came out of the bushes, he dragged as much dry brush and dead branches as he could possibly carry. By the time the others returned, he'd built four fire piles. All he had to do now was light them.

When they finished the last one, the boys stood and watched
the fires belch out thick, black smoke.

His friends had found several different things made out of plastic. "It's amazing how people think the ocean is just another garbage dump," Tyler said.

"I found a tire," Tony reported, "but I need help to drag it out of the sand." All three sprinted in the direction Tony pointed. Soon that smoke-maker was sitting in the middle of the largest fire, like the centerpiece on the table of the biggest birthday party Tony had ever given.

"Great," Sam announced. "We're ready to light the fires." One-by-one he placed a hot coal at the base of the dried leaves and twigs. And one-by-one, small flames eventually burst into roaring blazes. When they finished the last one, the boys stood and watched the fires belch out thick, black smoke.

"It looks like one of those war films," Tony said.

"This *is* like a war," Sam answered, "us against them. Okay, let's go hide in the jungle and see what happens."

They crept back into the thick plants like special op forces on a secret mission. Sam had found a perfect hiding spot while he collected all the firewood. They crouched down into a place where three large rocks stuck out of the sand. A dead tree had fallen across them, creating a perfectly hidden space. They grabbed a few more branches and placed them over any openings they found.

"Hey, I wish you'd found this earlier. We could have used it for our shelter," Tyler complained.

"If it isn't a shelter now, what *would* you call it?" Tony grumbled.

"Well, at least we wouldn't have had to waste all that time building our hut . . . a hut we just tore apart, I'd like to remind you."

After hiding for a time, it seemed to Sam like they had been in their secret place for hours. Unfortunately, the watch had quit working so it was impossible to know for sure. Just then, all three boys heard it at the same time. There was no mistake; the rumble of large boat motors raced closer and closer. Then, they mysteriously stopped.

"Hey," Tyler said to Tony, "I thought you said you knew all about their boats."

"I do."

"Then would you like to explain how they got 'em going again?"

"It isn't possible. I threw their wires in the water. I don't understand."

"Shhh," Sam whispered. "Like we thought before, maybe they keep everything they need out here for emergencies."

"That must be it," Tony said, defending himself.

"Let's just be quiet," Sam whispered.

For the next few minutes, all they could hear was how loud their breathing sounded. And Sam's heart pounded hard and fast like before. But the next sounds they heard made Sam's body become completely rigid and cold, like the fish he'd seen on the docks all laid out on ice. It sent a shiver through him so strong he shook uncontrollably.

"You okay?" Tony asked.

"No . . . I . . . am . . . not!" Sam sputtered.

It was clear someone was coming toward them. "I sure hope those are monkeys," Tyler squeaked.

The boys could clearly hear breaking branches on the ground being crushed under large, heavy feet. Now they even heard voices and the sounds of people pushing past leaves and branches on the trees not far from where the boys hid.

"I don't think those are monkeys," Tony whispered.

Huddled together and shaking all over, the boys waited for what surely would be the end. Sam clenched his fists, put his head down, and shut his eyes tight. He even clamped his teeth together like two halves of a clamshell.

"Hey!" a booming voice commanded, "You

in there. Come out where we can see you!"

Sam was sure he had stopped breathing all together. "Please be a dream. Please be a dream," he groaned.

"I said, come out!"

Sam and his friends crawled out from the safety of their hiding place, ready to accept the worst. They knew those scary men had finally found them.

Now what?

CHAPTER 15

Rescued!

Sam was too afraid to look at first, so he kept his eyes closed. But, as Tyler and Tony crawled out behind him, Tyler exclaimed, "Hey, where did you guys come from?"

"Yeah," Tony added. "And how'd you find us?"

One of the men chuckled. "All we had to do was follow your footprints in the sand from the beach, right to your hideout."

What a stupid thing to ask, Sam thought. *And why didn't I think to cover our tracks?* He pounded his fist in the dirt.

"We regularly patrol this place," another man answered. "We needed to know what was going on out here before we made our move."

"But nobody expected to find a bunch of boys out here," a third man added.

That's when Sam decided to open his eyes and see who they were talking to. In front of him stood the best sight he could have imagined. These men weren't dressed in black, they wore navy blue windbreakers. Some of the men looking around the area had DEA printed in big letters on the back. On others he saw the letters FBI.

"Hey," he exclaimed, "you're on our side!"

"Yes we are, but I just have one question for you."

"What's that?"

"What are you boys doing on Lost Island, and how did you get out here?"

Tony shook his head. "Do you want the long version, or the short one?" he asked.

"Let's try the short one."

"Well, you see, sir," Sam began. "We went out diving off a catamaran the day of the big storm."

"You mean with all the weather warnings you still went out?"

"We didn't hear them," Tyler said with a shrug.

A much larger man stepped forward. He pulled a piece of paper from his shirt pocket. "So tell me," he began, "would one of you be Tony?"

Tony took a half step backward, pointed to his chest, swallowed real hard, and said, "Uh, that'd be me."

"Your dad is very angry with you, young man. He told us to bring his boat back as soon as we found it...*if* we found it."

"Well," Tony said, "if you do find the rest of it, that won't do me much good."

"What does that mean?"

"Um, it means that it went to the bottom in pieces during the storm." Then Tony started crying. Sam didn't think he'd ever see that happen.

The big man looked at his paper again. "And

which one of you is Tyler?"

"Oh, man," he said with a squeak, "you wrote my name down?"

"Your father is very worried about you, son."

"You mean my mother, don't you? Or do you have us confused?" Tyler looked over to Sam.

"Oh, she's definitely worried too, but it's your dad who's been the most upset."

"Are you sure you got the right guy?"

The man gave Tyler a penetrating stare. "You're talking to the FBI."

Tyler looked down. "Oh, sorry."

The agent looked at his list again and then back up to where Sam stood. "Then you must be Sam."

Sam felt his throat tighten. "Yes, sir."

"Well, Sam. All I can tell you is you're gonna be in a heap of trouble when you get home."

"Yeah, don't I know it."

The man turned back to Tony. "Since it was

your dad's marina, and his boat, I'm assuming you know a little about sailing. Why don't you tell us what happened."

"Well . . . see . . . we came out to go diving, and we did that. Only I didn't listen to the radio for weather reports. Then this humongous storm came up out of nowhere."

"It was just like he said," Tyler added as he looked at Tony.

"I was trying to call the Coast Guard when a big wave, bigger than I've ever seen before, swamped the cabin and shorted out the radio."

Tyler put his hands as far apart as he could stretch. "You guys wouldn't believe how big that thing was—bigger than a house!"

"After that, it was all up to the storm," Tony said. "The boat broke apart and that's how we ended up here. I'm not exactly sure *how* that happened because we were all asleep until the next morning."

"Uh huh," the man said. "And then you set all these fires to signal for help?"

"Not exactly," Sam interrupted.

"Well, then?"

"That was to confuse those other guys."

"Other guys?"

"Yeah." Sam pointed back toward the jungle. "The guys dressed in black who are hiding on the other side of the island."

"Tell us about them."

"Well, let's see. They have these two super fast black boats."

Sam noticed the FBI agent seemed more interested in what he had to say. "Do the boats, by any chance, have sharks' faces painted on them?"

Tyler's eyes widened. "Yeah, with blood on the teeth and everything." Then he shuddered. Again his eyes blinked for a few seconds.

"We've been tracking those guys for a long time, but they've always been able to outrun our boats."

"You should see the engines on those babies," Tony said.

"A couple times we almost caught them," the agent continued, "but they disappeared."

"Well, we know where they go," Sam said with pride.

"You do? Where?"

"Have you ever seen the cove on the other side?"

"Of course," the man said, sounding impatient.

"They have these special bushes that open and close."

"Like a water garage," Tyler told them.

"They park the boats behind them and close 'em up again just like doors."

The agent took off his cap and rubbed a hand through his short hair. "Well, I'll be," the man exclaimed. He pulled a small radio out of his jacket pocket and barked out several orders. Some of it was in code. Sam looked over to Tony and Tyler who simply shrugged back. But they could clearly hear the sound of larger boat motors starting up in the distance, then speeding away around one side of the island.

"One more thing," Sam added.

The man turned back to him. "What's that?"

"Those shark boats aren't going anywhere."

"They aren't?" the man asked with raised eyebrows. "And why's that?"

Sam pointed to Tony. "Because my friend pulled out all the wires and threw them in the water."

"You did that?"

Tony's chest puffed way out. "Yes, yes, sir."

"Stunning!" The man got back on his radio and relayed the information to his men who were streaking toward the cove.

"But they do have a bunch of little rubber boats with small motors," Sam added. "If your big boats stay at the opening to the cove, they won't be able to get out."

The big man pointed to another of his men. "You boys go with Agent Owen over there. He has a boat waiting to take you back to port." He relayed another radio message about the small boats.

"But what about those men?" Tony asked in protest.

"We'll take care of them. No matter what they try to do, they can't hide from the FBI."

The boys were escorted toward the water. A large, rubber boat belonging to the agents sat on the beach, half on the sand, and half in the water. From there, it was easy to see a big Coast Guard cutter waiting offshore in deeper water. They'd never ridden on one of those before, and the boys chattered with excitement.

Safely on the Coast Guard boat and slicing through the water toward home, Sam thought about what the man had said. If no one could hide from the FBI, how much more was God able to see what he was doing. And when he did the wrong things, how did Sam think he could get away with it? One of the things his father liked to tell him was, "Character is what a guy does when no one is looking." He'd told Sam it was easy to do the right thing when other people could see him.

When the cutter neared Harper's Inlet, Sam felt both excited and afraid at the same time to see his parents.

Their boat operator got on his radio and told the officers on the dock to expect them in twenty minutes. "And make sure a police officer calls the boys' parents to have them waiting at the dock," he ordered.

Twenty minutes, Sam thought. His stomach felt like it sank to the deck. *In just twenty minutes, I'm gonna wish I was dead.* He went to one of the other men on his boat and asked, "Do you know anything about those guys we saw back on the island?"

"What do you want to know?"

"Who they are and what they're doing out there."

"Those are runners."

Sam tilted his head to one side. "Runners?"

"Every so often, a freighter calls them on the radio. We could intercept the calls, but by the time we arrived, the ship was back up to full steam, and the black boats were gone."

"Don't you use helicopters?"

"Sure, but the shark boats would come speeding out from Lost Island, load a bunch of boxes, and speed back to the island before we could scramble our pilots."

"Do you know what was in the boxes?"

"Drugs. Pure, uncut cocaine. Millions and millions of dollars worth. When they knew things had cooled down again and we weren't cruising around looking for them, they'd speed into port, drop the stuff off to their contact, and be gone again."

"And no one saw them?"

"Usually they did that part at night."

"Pretty smart," Tony said. "Black boats at night. Who'd see them?"

"Pretty dumb if you ask me," the man argued. "Those drugs cause nothing but pain. Just think of the people whose lives are ruined by that garbage. Also dumb because they thought they could stay under cover and never get caught. How stupid."

"So what we did, it was a good thing, right?" Sam asked.

The man thought for a moment. Then he looked at Sam. "Yes and no."

"What's the no part?" Tony asked.

"You went out in bad weather, didn't ask anyone, didn't tell anyone, and you lost your boat."

Tony looked down at the deck and let out a long, deep breath. "So tell me about the yes part."

"Truth is, this is a really big day for both the DEA and the FBI. It'll make some nice headlines for my boss, that's for sure. And it will give us more money to fight the battle down here."

"Money?" Tyler asked.

"You boys have no idea how much cash and equipment was just found in their hideout. We get to sell their boats too," he said with a smile.

"So our parents should be proud of us, not

mad, right?" Sam asked.

"That's something you'll have to take up with them. I just know I wouldn't want to be in your spot right about now."

After he said that, the main dock of the marina came into view. "I never thought that place could look so crummy," Tony muttered.

"I never thought I'd be afraid to see my own parents," Sam complained.

"Hey," Tyler said. "I think I see *both* my parents." Then he waved like he was returning as a hero from some great naval battle.

Sam couldn't figure out why anyone would want to wave at the very people who were about to dish out some of the worst punishment the boys had ever seen.

Their boat eased up to the side of the dock. The operator moved the gear lever into reverse and gunned his engines to bring them to a final stop. Even before the ropes could be secured, the boys' parents practically attacked the boat, trying to get to their sons.

"We thought you were gone forever," Tony's mother sobbed.

"Dad, I'm so sorry about the boat," Tony said.

"Boat? Are you kidding? I can always get another boat, but you, you couldn't *possibly* be replaced." His parents squeezed him until it looked like they might smother the boy.

Sam hurried to his parents. "I don't know what to say. I guess I'm grounded 'til forever."

"What you did was wrong, no doubt about it," his father said. "But I think you probably learned more out there in the past few days than any punishment could teach you."

Sam's eyes darted from one of his parents to the other and back again. "You mean it?"

"We sure do," his mother added as the three of them pulled together for their group hug. From where Sam stood, he was able to see Tyler.

At first, Tyler and his father just stood and looked at each other. Then they came together with such force, Sam thought both of them would wind up in the water.

"Hey, buddy," his father began. "I thought I'd lost you for good." Then he squeezed him even harder.

"Dad," Tyler choked, "you're hurting me."

His father eased up on his grip. "I'm sorry, it's just that the idea you might be seriously hurt or dead caused me to start thinking about some of the things I'd been doing. I haven't been very nice to your mom."

He turned toward his wife and continued, "If she'll give me the chance to prove it, in time, I want to show both of you that I can be a good father and husband. I thought I could cover up some things, but now I see how foolish I've been."

Tyler and his parents hugged and cried together softly. A few minutes later, Sam went to Tyler and asked, "Do you think your parents could start coming to church with us?"

"Oh, we would love to," his mother sighed

with joy.

"Then, I'll see you guys in Sunday school," he said to his friends.

Sam and his parents turned to leave the dock when they heard a message from the radio of the Coast Guard boat that had brought the boys in.

"Operation Rip Tide to base, Rip Tide to base, over."

"Base, over."

"Prepare to receive prisoners. Rip Tide, out."

"We got 'em," one of the officers announced.

Everyone on the dock cheered, and the boys jumped up and down and celebrated with them.

Because of the seriousness of the drug crimes involved, the boys were not allowed to be photographed or interviewed so no one could find them later.

"You boys can't ever tell anyone about this," a DEA officer instructed. "You wouldn't be safe if you did."

"Great," Tony said. "We solve the crime of the century and nobody will ever know it."

"Not even our friends?" Tyler asked.

The officer simply shook his head.

"One thing I learned," Sam told his parents. "I'm never going to try to hide anything from you or God again. It's just not worth it."

Then Tony's mother clapped her hands for attention. "We've planned a big celebration cookout for you boys," she announced, "with hamburgers and everything."

"Ohhh," Tony groaned as he held his stomach. "I'd do anything for a hamburger right now."

Sam thought that stomach looked a bit smaller than the day they'd left for their little diving expedition. A sly smile came to his face. "Tony, you said you'd do anything?"

He nodded as he looked over to Sam. "Anything," he groaned in agony.

"Would you eat a can of . . . beans?"

"Please," Tyler cried, "tell me there won't be any beans at the cookout."

"No beans," his father promised. "But I did buy the biggest watermelon you ever saw," he announced proudly.

The boys turned and looked to each other. "Not a *watermelon*," Tyler said.

"I sure hope it's seedless," Sam added.

Then all three boys smiled at each other and laughed.

Tony whispered to his friends as he shook his head, "I don't ever want to see another watermelon, ever! No watermelon candy. No watermelon gum, or fruit rolls, or anything that even reminds me of the stupid fruit. In fact, the next guy who dares to speak the W word is gonna get it." He slammed a fist into his other hand.

A sly smile slowly spread across Sam's face. He looked, first at Tyler, then to Tony. He took in a deep breath. Then he yelled, "*Watermelon*," and ran toward the shed where he'd hidden his bike. But it wasn't there.

The other boys almost caught up to him as he darted to one side and headed for the end of the dock. Just as Sam reached a grassy area, Tyler caught him with a flying tackle around the ankles. The two tumbled to the ground and Tony joined them as they tussled, kicking, laughing, and rolling in the grass.

Their parents came to the end of the dock and just stood there watching their sons. "My, my," Tony's mother remarked. "Of all the things they missed out there on that terrible island, who would have guessed . . . *watermelon?*"

That made the boys roar even louder as they continued laughing and rolling around on the ground like the best friends they had just become.

After what they had all been through together, these three guys knew they were going to be friends for a long, long time, maybe even for the rest of their lives.

Finally the fight was over, and Sam sat up

in the grass. He looked around at the dock, the marina, and back toward his friends who were completely out of breath.

That's when he noticed a broken-down, old boat sitting up out of the water, next to one of the other docks. "What a wreck," he whispered. *But a guy sure could have some great adventures if he fixed the thing up*, he thought. He looked over to his friends again. *I sure hope I get to live here for at least two more years*, he thought, *maybe five*. He paused a little longer and then whispered, "Maybe I'll never have to move again."

- The End -

*BE SURE TO READ THE NEXT
SAM COOPER ADVENTURE...*

"Hey you guys," Tony pointed and said, "have you seen that sorry excuse for a boat?"

"I noticed it when we came back from Lost Island," Sam said.

The boat was badly weathered, with broken windows, and in need of more than a simple coat of paint. A short, stocky man emerged from below. He looked almost as weathered as the deck he stood on.

Sam, Tony, and Tyler didn't know it yet, but they were about to find themselves smack in the middle of their next adventure—discovering *CAPTAIN JACK'S TREASURE*!

Chocolate Dessert

1 ½ sticks of butter (softened)
1 ½ cups all-purpose flour
1 ½ cups chopped pecans

Mix butter, flour, and pecans. Press into a 9 x 13-inch baking pan.

Bake at 350 degrees for 15 to 20 minutes or until light brown. Let cool to room temperature.

Mix (8-ounce) cream cheese (softened), 1 cup powdered sugar, and 1 cup Cool Whip and spread over cooled crust

Beat at low speed 2 packages of instant chocolate pudding with 3cups of milk for 2 minutes and quickly pour over the cream cheese layer. When the pudding is firm, spread the rest of the Cool Whip over the top.

Refrigerate over night or at least 6 hours.
Yield: 12 servings

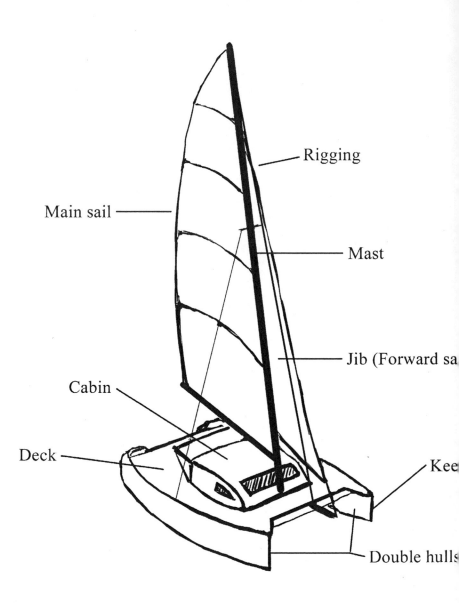

Rigging

Main sail

Mast

Jib (Forward sa

Cabin

Deck

Kee

Double hulls

CATAMARANS

Sam, Tony, and Tyler used a different kind of sailboat for their first diving adventure. Most sailboats have a single hull that goes deep into the water, to help keep it from tipping over in the wind. But their boat was a *catamaran*.

A *catamaran* is a type of boat with two hulls joined by a frame. The word *catamaran* comes from the Tamil language in

India and it means "logs bound together" or "tied wood."

An English adventurer, William Dampier, sailed the world in the 1690s. He is the first to write in English about a kind of boat that he saw there. In 1697 he wrote, "...they call them *catamarans*. These are but one log, or two, sometimes of a sort of light wood . . . so small, they carry but one man."

Even though the name *catamaran* came from Tamil, the boats we see today are from the South Pacific. English sailors simply applied the name *catamaran* to the swift sail and paddle boats made out of two widely separated logs that were used by the Polynesians to travel between islands. The *catamaran* remained unknown in the West for 200 years.

Although sailing a traditional sailboat and the *catamaran* may be similar, there are differences. *Catamarans* are more difficult to turn into the wind. The *catamaran* has a faster speed, and it is less likely to capsize. The reasons they are faster than single hulled boats include their lighter weight. Also, the wider distance from one side of the boat to the other gives a *catamaran* more stability. And finally, the *catamaran* sail is more likely to stay straight, while the sail of a monohull would usually lean over in the wind.

Recent developments have brought us *powered-catamarans* that don't use a sail, and *mega-catamarans* that are built for luxury yachts, all the way up to large *catamaran car ferries* and naval vessels.

Today, *catamarans* are the fastest growing part of the boating industry.

Even though the *catamaran* is a stable sailboat, it was no match for the powerful storm that Sam, Tony, and Tyler battled.

Green jungle grass and palm branches

Live tree

Vines to lash wood together

Door

Live tree

Log frame

Dead branches to form walls and floor

Stilt to keep hut off the ground

How to make a shelter

If you ever find yourself stranded in the woods, on a jungle island like these boys, in the snow, or anywhere that leaves you out in the sun, wind, rain, or snow, one of the most important things you need is shelter. A shelter not only keeps you out of the elements, it also helps to protect you from animals.

The kind of shelter you build, will depend on where you are, and what items you have available.

Hikers may have a poncho or hammock with them. The hammock can be strung between two trees in order to keep the hiker off the ground. In colder weather, it will be important to build a fire. In this case, the shelter would be built on the ground. Sticks tied together with vines or rope can provide a frame. The poncho, or branches and plants can be used to make a top and back to the shelter. This shelter is called a lean to. With a fire in front, most animals will stay away.

When someone is lost in the mountains, digging a snow cave is a good form of shelter. In this case, it's best to find a snowdrift, or deep snow. This can be hollowed out by digging with your hands. Even though you'll still be cold, the snow cave will keep you out of the wind, falling temperatures, and snow.

Sam, Tony, and Tyler had landed on an island. They had no idea what kinds of animals or insects might be there too. So Sam decided to build a shelter, off of the ground, like one he'd seen on TV.

First the boys searched for long, round pieces of wood along the beach. These were used for two corners of their shelter. Sam chose a spot that already had two trees standing close together, so those formed the other two corners. They placed a center pole in position to make their hut's floor stronger. Sam sharpened one end of each pole with the ax, and then set them in the sand. Next, he used vines that he'd found in the jungle to tie other sticks together to make the frame. The floor was built from stronger sticks and it sat above the sand. This meant that snakes, bugs, and small animals couldn't easily bother the boys while they slept. He used smaller sticks for the top and sides of their hut. Next they gathered palm branches, and other broad, leafy plants to cover the roof. This was done by placing the leaves in rows, starting from the top of the roof, and tying each section with more vines so the wind couldn't blow them away. When the leafy plants and palm branches had been layered, they would keep out most of the rain. Sticks tied to the sides of their hut kept out the wind. Sam built the final side and left an opening just big enough for them to get in and out. The finishing touch was to gather dry grass and spread it over the floor for soft beds.

All the boys hoped now was that nothing would climb up into their shelter after dark.

 **Max Elliot Anderson** grew up as a reluctant reader. After surveying the market, he sensed the need for action-adventures and mysteries for readers eight and up, especially boys.

Mr. Anderson was a producer of the nationally televised PBS special, *Gospel at the Symphony*, that was nominated for an Emmy, and won a Grammy for the double album soundtrack. He won a best cinematographer award for the film, Pilgrim's Progress, which was the first feature film in which Liam Neeson had a staring role. He has produced, directed, or shot over 500 national television commercials for True Value Hardware Stores.

Mr. Anderson owns *The Market Place*, a client-based video production company for medical and industrial clients. His productions have taken him all over the world including India, New Guinea, Europe, Canada, and across the United States.

Using his extensive experience in the production of motion pictures, videos, and television commercials, Mr. Anderson brings the same visual excitement and heart-pounding action to his stories. With the exception of the Sam Cooper Adventures, each book has completely different characters, setting, and plot. Young readers have reported that reading one of Mr. Anderson's books is like being in an exciting or scary movie.

Author Web Site: www.maxbooks.9k.com
Books for Boys Blog: booksandboys.blogspot.com/

Mr. Anderson is listed in WHO'S WHO in Finance and Industry, Entertainment, Advertising, The Midwest, Emerging Leaders in America, The World, and WHO'S WHO In America (1999 - present)

Holly Heisey - artist/illustrator

Her work has appeared in various local and national venues. She trained in fine art for ten years before branching out to illustration, and now works in the new wave of digital illustrators. Holly also enjoys playing piano and guitar and writing science fiction stories. You can see Holly's work at her website:

http://hollyheisey.com

Watch for other titles from:

Port Yonder Press

The Sam Cooper Adventure Series
Captain Jack's Treasure
River Rampage
by Max Elliot Anderson

The Caribbean Chronicles
Volumes 1-3
by Eddie Jones

And more!
www.PortYonderPress.com

LaVergne, TN USA
25 July 2010
190803LV00001B/4/P

9 781935 600022